Garry Disher grew up on a wheat and wool farm in South Australia. He has an MA in Australian History and has lived, worked and travelled in England, Italy, Israel, the USA and southern Africa. In 1978 he was awarded a creative writing fellowship to Stanford University, where he wrote his first collection of short stories. Garry worked as a writing lecturer between the years 1980 and 1988, before becoming a full-time writer. He has published over fifty books, including short story collections, literary novels, writers' handbooks and award-winning crime thrillers and children's titles.

LOTHIAN CLASSICS
by Garry Disher

Eva's Angel
From Your Friend, Louis Deane
Good One, Erm
Maddie Finn
Ratface
Restless
The Apostle Bird
The Bamboo Flute
The Divine Wind
Two-way Cut
Walk Twenty, Run Twenty

GARRY DISHER

FROM YOUR FRIEND, LOUIS DEANE

LOTHIAN

A Lothian Children's Book

This edition published in Australia and New Zealand in 2019
by Hachette Australia
(an imprint of Hachette Australia Pty Limited)
Level 17, 207 Kent Street, Sydney NSW 2000
www.hachettechildrens.com.au

First published in 2000 by Hodder Children's Books

10 9 8 7 6 5 4 3 2 1

A catalogue record for this book is available from the National Library of Australia

ISBN 978 0 7344 1932 3 (paperback)

Cover design by Grace West
Author photograph courtesy L. Healey
Typeset by Bookhouse, Sydney
Printed and bound in Australia by McPherson's Printing Group

The paper this book is printed on is certified against the Forest Stewardship Council® Standards. McPherson's Printing Group holds FSC® chain of custody certification SA-COC-005379. FSC® promotes environmentally responsible, socially beneficial and economically viable management of the world's forests.

For Sam and Milly

ONE

We always hurt the ones we love. Discuss.

Easy. The easiest essay topic he'd ever been given. Louis Deane scribbled it into his exercise book, filed out of the classroom with the other Year 8s, grabbed his bag and crossed the yard to the gates of Bass Beach Secondary College, letting the sentences fall into place in his head:

Once upon a time there was a happy family. They lived in the city. The mother and the father loved their children. Then one fine day, they uprooted them from their neighbours and friends and took them to live somewhere else. 'We're leaving the rat race,' they said. 'We're moving to a town on the coast. You'll love it there.'

But the children didn't love it there. They didn't know anyone and had no friends and didn't fit in. The other kids were hoons and there was nothing to do. The children felt betrayed…

Louis stamped along, through the gate and down High Street, stamping the words out, one by one. It was a chilly midwinter day, well suited to his mood.

Seven long months went by, and—

A bulky shoulder knocked him flying. 'Whoops! Sorry, Claypot.'

It was Craven, his chief tormentor in Year 8. As usual, Bird was with him. They were clones of each other: squat and thick. Thick bodies, Louis thought, thick heads, and thick, hot pimples. Now both were brushing him down, feigning concern. 'Poor Kilnhead. Are you okay?'

Never his real names, 'Louis' or 'Deane', but always some snide reference to the shop his father had opened, Bass Beach Pottery. There had never been a pottery in Bass Beach before. Only a supermarket, bank, garage, Chinese takeaway, hopeless video library, hardware store, newsagent and post office, and a tiny private hospital. No one ever bought the pottery that Louis' father made. To the locals, the pottery was a joke and the Deanes were outsiders and would always be—even if we lived here for a hundred years, Louis thought. Not that he wanted to be an *in*sider.

He tried to jerk away from Craven and Bird, but they crowded him against the peeling picket fence around the Catholic church. 'Where you going, Potboy?'

'Home.'

'Yeah, right. You live in the opposite direction, dick brain.'

'Haircut,' Louis admitted finally.

It was Friday. Craven sneered. 'Which babe are you taking out this weekend?'

Louis didn't have a girlfriend, and they knew it, just as they—and their parents—knew everything about everybody. It was that kind of town.

'No one.'

'Didn't think so. What kind of cut?'

Louis was slowly training his hair. He wanted

to wear it surfie style eventually, straight and long and swinging clean, but it still had a way to go. 'I need a trim,' he said, expecting further sneers.

But there was a flicker of interest in Craven's heavy, mournful face. He wore his hair long, but it was always tangled and unwashed looking. Louis could smell him: an odour of sweat and cigarettes caught in the school jumper and blazer that strained over his short, barrelly torso.

He glanced at Bird, at the strength in Bird's solid chest and short bowed legs. Bird unconsciously patted himself: his hair was long, stiff, puffed-up, dirty yellow in colour, and as daggy as Craven's.

Louis came to a terrible realisation: his own hair was only a few centimetres, a shampoo and a combing better looking than Craven's and Bird's.

'Who cuts it?' Bird demanded.

'The windmill man.'

Craven folded his arms. 'My mum cuts mine.'

Louis stopped himself from saying: *Yeah, looks like it, too.*

Bird said, 'My sister cuts mine. She's got a certificate.'

They stood back, as though announcing a victory over him. Louis retreated one step, then another, and another. Then he ran, hearing them cackle behind him.

He headed along High Street. He knew why they'd targeted him when he'd arrived in Bass Beach seven months earlier—because he was a new kid—but why were they keeping it up? Bored out of their little brains? Because he got good marks? Because his parents were hippies? Or maybe, Louis thought, they want to make me over into their image. He shuddered.

At the corner of High and Whiting Streets, he risked a glance over his shoulder. All clear. They'd switched their attention to the new kid.

She was a good target: she'd only started at the school that week, and was weird looking. On her first day, Old Valentine had warned her about the school's uniform code. He'd flicked at the offending items in her dress: 'Clear nail polish only, please, no nose studs, no eyeshadow, no neon hair, and is that tattoo genuine? If so, please cover it up.'

It was a tiny butterfly, just above her collarbone. The neon hair was gone the next day, and the stud, eyeshadow and nail polish, but the butterfly was still visible inside her collar. Louis had told himself at the time, 'They'll wear you down,' but hadn't given her a thought since then. He couldn't remember her name. He was too lost in his own misery to care about some new kid.

He watched now as Craven and Bird spun her around and pushed her back and forth between them and snatched her bag to rummage in it. She was standing up to them bravely.

Louis caught himself thinking: Maybe now they'll leave *me* alone.

TWO

He turned away and headed down Whiting Street. Mr Chatters lived at the end, next to the level crossing. The sign on his gate said: *Roly Chatterton Windmill Repairs Odd Jobs Barbering Done.* Bass Beach was that kind of town. A sleepy, rundown, dead-end little place in a forgotten corner of the Bay, where men like Mr Chatters fixed windmills, painted roofs and cut hair for a living, and fishermen's widows reared wild Year 8 kids, took in sewing and gave home perms in their kitchens. When Louis' father had first tried to sell Louis the idea of moving to Bass Beach he'd said, 'You'll like it—a town where decent, hard-working people make do as best they can,' but as far as Louis was concerned Bass Beach was populated by thugs and halfwits.

His father had changed his tune a little since then. Just the other night he'd sighed, 'I don't think Bass Beach is ready for a pottery.'

So why, Louis demanded now, as he stamped along the street, *don't you sell up and take us back where we belong?* He thought again of the essay topic. *We always hurt the ones we love...*

He pushed open Mr Chatters' squeaky gate and ducked and weaved through the overgrown garden to the flyscreened back porch. A rotting, sun-faded sign tacked to the screen door said: *Please Enter Haircuts*.

Louis knocked and entered. It was cool and dim inside Mr Chatters' back porch. Even on a cloudless day very little natural light found its way in to warm the bones, for the flyscreen was caked with rust and dust, fruit trees and oleanders crowded the backyard, and the heavy green linoleum and bubbled brown paint absorbed the muted rays of the sun. When

Louis had first told his mother about the darkness, she'd said that Mr Chatters belonged to a generation who would never fit a 100 watt bulb when 40 watts would do.

Mr Chatters was cutting Sergeant Penny's hair, a squashed, damp, greyish narrow fag bobbing in the corner of his mouth. He jerked at Louis to sit and wait.

Louis liked waiting on Mr Chatters' cracked, horsehairy sofa, flipping through the magazines piled next to it—the kinds of magazines that were never allowed at home. The radio was always on, playing a mix of golden oldies and latest releases, and it was clear that Mr Chatters paid attention, for he knew all the songs and who sang them. Louis would listen, half tuned to the radio and half to the yarns of Mr Chatters, but sometimes the afternoon train would growl past on the level crossing, just metres away from the house, and Louis would feel it in his feet and his thighs, a faint, forewarning tremor as it approached, and everyone would freeze—Mr Chatters with his brilliant clacking scissors, a sheeted client in the creaking bentwood kitchen chair, Louis with a magazine spread open upon his knees—until that train seemed to mow them down and power on into the distance.

When Sergeant Penny had paid and gone, Mr Chatters shook out the sheet and said, 'G'day, Lou. Same as before?'

Louis paused. This was his sixth haircut in Bass Beach. They were upkeep haircuts, to keep his hair symmetrical while it grew out. Luckily Mr Chatters had twigged to what was being asked of him right from the start. Louis had been expecting a daggy setup, an old man with fixed ideas, but Mr Chatters had photos of all kinds of styles pinned to his wall and always spoke to Louis as an equal, not as a kid. Louis liked him. Mr Chatters was about the only person in Bass Beach who made him feel welcome.

'Just a trim?' Mr Chatters persisted.

The idea hit Louis out of nowhere: *No, cut it all off.* He sat wordlessly, the pressure building in his skull. Craven and Bird, with their long, daggy hair. His own father, growing his hair and tying it back in a ponytail. They're all submerging me, he thought. I'll disappear, melt into this town as though I'd always belonged here.

'Cat got your tongue, Lou?'

'Cut it all off,' Louis said.

Mr Chatters whistled. 'Are you sure? Midwinter, I don't want you catching your death.'

Louis liked that, Mr Chatters showing concern instead of coming on all heavy or saying he'd better check with the oldies first. 'Cut it as short as you can,' Louis said. 'Buzz-cut.'

'Well, you're the boss,' Mr Chatters said, and he began to cut. He was a talker, commenting, yarning and asking questions in time with the deft shaping motions of his hands. 'How's your old man? Selling any pots?'

'No,' Louis said.

The scissors clacked. 'How about you? Making any friends yet?'

Mr Chatters seemed genuinely to care, so Louis answered him truthfully, the words building to a flood, laying out all of his pain and loneliness. He twisted violently in his chair. 'I hate it here. I don't fit in, I'll never fit in, I don't even *want* to fit in. I get picked on, they make fun of my dad, everyone's a total nerd.'

The scissors didn't stop, but they did seem to grow thoughtful. 'I know the feeling. I've been here fifteen years and I still feel I'm on the outer.'

'You, too?'

'Came down here for the wife's health,' Mr Chatters explained. 'Some good sea air for her lungs. It suits her here, she's always been happy with her own company, but me, I need a good chinwag every now and then. It takes a while to get accepted, Lou. It isn't easy. Then again, you strike me as someone who has interests to fall back on, something to call your own, am I right?'

Louis confided in him about his love of reading, his favourite writer, Terry Pratchett, and the Terry Pratchett Web site he'd designed and uploaded onto the Internet.

'Huh,' Mr Chatters said. 'Above my head. But see, a lot of the kids in this place haven't got what you've got. I bet they're envious of you.'

Louis thought about that. It didn't seem likely. In fact, sometimes when he felt very low, he envied the other kids—wanted Craven and Bird and the others to accept him.

But he didn't tell Mr Chatters that. He listened as Mr Chatters went on: 'And there's one simple thing to keep in mind.'

'What?'

'You can always leave.'

'Yeah, right, I can just see my mum and dad letting me do that,' Louis said.

'I don't mean now. Don't be in a hurry. Make the most of things here, limited though they are. For example, have you got yourself a partner for the Polonaise yet?'

The Polonaise. A major yawn as far as Louis was concerned. He didn't even want to think about the Polonaise. It was a Bass Beach thing and therefore beneath his contempt—but he couldn't ignore it because the kids at school kept saying to him: 'Who's your partner? Got a partner yet?'

As Louis understood it, the Polonaise was a kind of dance, the high point of the school's Annual Ball, held in the shire hall on the last Friday of term before the September school break. Everyone went to the Ball, but only the school kids danced the Polonaise itself. Every kid in the school was expected to take part, and to dress up for it. The town demanded a serious commitment to the Ball and the Polonaise. The tradition went back generations and was unique to Bass Beach.

But it sounded daggy to Louis. The Polonaise wasn't so much a dance as a kind of stately march, with couples trailing one another up and down and around the dance floor. He preferred the mosh-pit atmosphere of the clubs he used to go to up in the city, back in the good old days.

'Not yet,' he said.

'Better get your skates on. The Ball's in six weeks time.'

'I know.'

Louis wondered if Mr Chatters might give him some advice, tell him who to ask or even how to get out of going to the Ball. It was not the sort of thing he could raise with anyone else in Bass Beach.

But at that moment, Mr Chatters stopped clacking his scissors. The front gate had squeaked. 'Ah, there she is,' he said.

Mrs Chatters? Louis wondered. The

Chattertons had no children of their own. He listened to the footsteps, tracking Mrs Chatters as she crunched along the side path to the back porch. He'd never seen Mrs Chatters. He'd scarcely even heard her before, apart from a creaking floorboard now and then, or the vacuum cleaner, or a broom knocking against a skirting board somewhere, deep inside the dark, dark house.

The screen door protested on its rusty hinges. This wasn't Mrs Chatters. It was the new kid. She dumped her schoolbag in the corner, accepted a kiss from Mr Chatters, and sat on the horsehair sofa, swinging her legs, glancing curiously at Louis. She didn't look as though she'd just been roughed up by Craven and Bird, and had, Louis realised, now that she was sitting barely two metres away from him, a lovely, clever, totally neat face.

THREE

'Hi, Louis,' she said.

Louis felt his face grow hot. What was her name? 'Hi.'

'Uncle Roly, can I please get something to eat?'

'Tilly, love, what's ours is yours.'

Tilly Chatterton, that was it.

She went through to the main part of the house, and came back with an apple and a novel. Louis glanced at the author's name: Terry Pratchett. He found himself saying, 'Top book. Really funny.'

She smiled as if to agree with him. Louis felt a tingle, a connection with her. 'I've got all Terry Pratchett's books,' he said, 'and I run a Terry Pratchett Web site.'

'Really?' she said.

'It gets a few hundred hits a month.'

'I'll have to log on and look at it.'

He watched her surreptitiously from the creaking chair as Mr Chatters continued to cut. She chewed the apple and read her book, but would glance across from time to time. Once, when she caught his gaze, she smiled, and his face grew hotter.

If the Chattertons had bought her a school uniform, did that mean she was going to be around for a while? Where were her parents?

Meanwhile, Mr Chatters' broad, ash-speckled torso was close to Louis' ear. The words came as a rumble deep inside it: 'Fine shaped head you've got, young Louis.'

Louis was embarrassed. He was aware of Tilly sizing him up. Had he done the wrong thing in having his hair shorn off? Would she screw up her face in disgust at the sight?

A feeling of panic began to grow in him. It

happened sometimes when he felt trapped, as if all of his senses were being crowded. There was the cotton sheet, shutting him down from neck to ankle; there was Tilly, who had him at a disadvantage; and there was Mr Chatters himself, dancing around the chair, his feet nimble, his eyes narrowed, the scissors' blades a blur in his massive hands.

Louis gulped. He badly needed air. Those hands: the palms were as solid as mallet heads, the fingers as tough as rope. They were hands the colour of hard work, and dirt, and burning solar rays.

Mr Chatters leaned to peer at Louis' left ear. The big head in close-up was whiskery, veined and seamed. The skin was as leathery and dry as a work boot. Dark hairs showed at the neck of an old shirt. Louis could smell Mr Chatters now, a compound of soap, shaving cream, hair oil, tobacco and perspiration—not unpleasant, but still Louis gasped and had to push Mr Chatters away.

Mr Chatters looked perplexed. 'Haven't finished yet, son.'

Louis breathed in and out heavily. The girl stared at him.

'It's all right, son,' Mr Chatters said gently, and he snapped off the radio in the middle of a Paul Kelly single, placed his huge, calming hands on Louis' temples, and said, 'Shhh.' Louis began to relax.

'Just a bit more off,' Mr Chatters said.

There was a flicker of concern in the girl's eyes. Louis looked away.

'Tilly, love, would you fetch Louis a glass of water, please?'

Louis watched her bang through the gloomy door at the end of the porch. He heard water gushing from a tap.

'Finished!' Mr Chatters said, whisking away the sheet and releasing drifts of cropped hair.

The big hands turned Louis' jaw this way and that. A broad, dry palm gently cupped the back of his skull. 'Beautifully shaped head,' Mr Chatters said. He coughed apologetically. 'That'll be five dollars, son.'

As Louis fished in his pocket, Tilly returned from the kitchen. He felt stupid, embarrassed, to be accepting a glass of water like this, in these circumstances. He was sure that both Tilly and Mr Chatters were laughing at him.

But he swallowed the water, coughed, and turned to go.

'See you around,' Tilly said.

Louis stopped and looked at the floor. 'See you.'

'Cool haircut.'

Louis said 'thanks' to the floor and left.

He was glad to be outside. The world seemed to expand to its normal size. He filled his lungs with air and stood for a while, where he couldn't be spied on.

In the muddy driveway stood an ancient Austin truck. It had a sun-faded red cabin, black wheel arches and a chrome ornament in the shape of a flying *A* on the end of the stubby bonnet. Never mind that the Austin had no working brakes or lights and had scraped every gatepost in the district; never mind that the springs showed tiredly through the seats and the doors were rusted out and a hot wind whistled through the holes in the floorpan, Mr Chatters loved his truck and kept the flying *A* polished and free of rust.

Louis stepped closer to the Austin and poked it with a finger. Hand-painted on both doors were the words: *Roly Chatterton Windmill Expert Bass Beach*. The tray of the truck—a few gappy, oily, rotting planks—listed beneath the weight of tool chests, chains, crowbars, iron fence droppers, and a badly welded rack of windmill rods and piping.

Brass, iron, copper—those were the other things that Mr Chatters smelt of, tasted of.

Who was Tilly? How did she fit in?

Louis made his way back to the street. He looked both ways. It was safe to leave.

FOUR

Louis turned left on High Street and slipped around the back of the shopping centre and toward home. The shopping centre was a dreary expanse of stunted or dead shrubs on tan-bark islands, a handful of family cars, a couple of cement benches and tables in one corner, and a yellow plastic swing and slide in another. Kids would hang out there after school, one or two of them desultorily toe-flipping their skateboards or wheel-standing on their bikes, the others smoking, giggling, staring about, or cramming fish and chips into their mouths. They had nowhere else to go, nothing else to do. There seemed to be two levels of ambition amongst them: those who couldn't wait to finish school and leave the district, and the majority who would one day find themselves married and living no more than a street away from where they'd grown up, and with kids at the same school they'd attended.

As Louis neared home, he could feel his feet slowing, slowing. The shingle for Bass Beach Pottery swung in the breeze that came in off the Bay. There were no customers' cars parked anywhere near the shop. There never were.

He stopped. He sat with his feet in the gutter. Between gaps in the mangroves on one arm of the Bay and the dunes and ti-trees on the other, was a narrow channel of water, marked by buoys. The Bay was known for its silt and shifting sandbars. Seabirds poked about, leaving fine webbed impressions in the mud. There was a refinery on the point. Chimney tops burned day and night.

This was the ugliest part of the Peninsula and Louis couldn't understand why, if his parents *had* to live here, they couldn't have chosen one of the prettier parts.

He supposed it had to do with money. There was supposed to be enough for living expenses and pocket money but he was always being told that there wasn't much capital left. Most had gone on buying the shop, the kiln, and a bush block with an old house on it, a few kilometres inland of Bass Beach. Louis' father intended to restore the house and move the family into it. The idea depressed Louis. Living in Bass Beach was isolation enough, but to live in a bush block outside of the town was worse.

The rest of the money had gone on funding his parents' re-run of their teens and early twenties —surfboards, a Harley Davidson motorbike, massage oils, candles, a guitar. They'd grown up in the city, been high school and university sweethearts, and had spent every summer on the surf beaches of the Peninsula, sleeping in a panel van or a tent.

After graduation they'd found jobs and bought a house in the city, got married, and had children, Louis and his elder sister, Meg. Louis had been happy in the city. The city was the centre of his existence. Things were easygoing at home and most of his friends lived within walking distance. He and Meg were encouraged to call their father Carl and their mother Steph, and were trusted to take themselves off to films or concerts, so long as they were home by about eleven at night. Last year Louis had moved up to secondary college with most of his friends, and it was a top school, with teachers who were relaxed about stuff like uniform.

But then it all went wrong. Within a short space of time, the Deanes had found themselves vulnerable to the worst aspects of city life. Meg was attacked on the train by a girl gang who snatched her laptop computer, and Steph was robbed at an automatic teller machine by a man who'd held a bloody syringe to her throat and told her he had AIDS.

Then it was Louis' turn. He was in an amusement parlour one Friday after school, playing a new strategy game, when he was nabbed by the police and told he'd been filmed in an alley, acting as the daily lookout for a heroin dealer. Carl was furious; Louis had never seen his father so furious, and had admired the way he went away and came back with evidence to demolish the police case. 'Here is my son's attendance record for the past year,' he'd shouted, waving Louis' home-room teacher's ledger in the air. 'I suggest you look again at your videotape.'

Steph losing her job, that was the final straw. The co-ordinator of a community placement program for kids, she'd arrived at work one day to find a termination offer in her pigeonhole. The program's funding had not been renewed. She was devastated, but began to look for other jobs, until one day she came home in tears, saying, 'Today I was told I'm too old. Too old? I'm only forty.'

It was all bad, but moving away from the city was the last thing Louis expected his parents would want to do. He was appalled when one day Carl and Steph beamingly called a family conference and announced, 'We've had enough. We're moving to the coast. You kids deserve better. We'll be self-sufficient. We won't need much. It's going to be great.'

As though the matter had been decided and

the kids had no say in it. Louis hated the eager look in their eyes.

That had been last October. By February the Deanes were living in Bass Beach, ninety minutes by train from the city. Now it was August, and Louis and Meg didn't think that things were better at all. Bass Beach was the arse-end of the known universe.

Louis got to his feet and dragged himself home. He scraped open the gate at the side of the shop. The family lived in a few rooms at the back. He edged past his mother's car, feeling the warmth of the engine inside the bonnet. Steph had found a part-time job in the shire council's crèche, the only job that came anywhere near matching her qualifications.

He stared gloomily at his father's kiln. It sat in the backyard between the clothesline and the woodheap. Today the kiln was giving off waves of heat: Carl had been firing pots again, pots and vases and coffee mugs and bread crocks to add to those that sat unsold in the shop window. Meanwhile the Harley Davidson and the surfboards were gathering dust on the back verandah. So much for regaining lost youth, Louis thought.

He went inside. He could hear murmurs coming from beyond the door to the shop, and knew that Carl and Steph were in there, but he didn't want to talk to them. The only person he wanted to talk to was Meg, who had the gift of making everything seem better.

FIVE

To ease their pain and disappointment, Louis and Meg would talk. They would talk through mealtimes, during the ads on TV, while idling along the beach on weekends, whenever they encountered each other in a school corridor, and in Meg's bedroom after school. If they were alone, they'd speak in normal tones; if not, they'd speak softly, in hurried snatches, like spies or thieves. They huddled together when they talked. The talking comforted them, and it kept their memories fresh. They were like historians for each other, remembering their old friends, their old house and street in the city, their old school. They laughed a little longingly about the things that had pleased them in the past. Nothing in their present measured up, they had no one but each other, and Louis thought that if he didn't have Meg in his life, then he'd forget his past and not have much of a future.

He found her bent over her sketchbook, deftly adding pencil strokes to a drawing of the misshapen tree that had sat in the backyard of their house in the city. She was plugged into her portable CD player. Wordlessly she removed one earplug, held it out to him, and returned to her drawing. He listened for a while. The Cowboy Junkies. They had gone to see the band at the Palais last year, back in the good old days when they were happy, back where there were gigs at stadiums and concert halls almost every day of the week.

Meg rolled onto her back. She was fifteen. She was wearing a tiny amethyst nose stud, three gold rings in the lobe of her left ear, and a dunny-ring choker—a black rubber ring designed to seal sewerage pipes but available in any hardware store for fifty cents. She'd worn it to school once and been told that it transgressed the uniform code, so now she only wore it after school and on weekends. Her hair had a hacked-about look, dyed coal black. She liked to wear black and purple velvet whenever she could, with black tights and black Doc Martens boots. To the people of Bass Beach, it was a hard and unforgiving look. Only Louis knew her gentleness.

She switched off the CD. 'Hey, really like your hair.'

Louis went to the mirror. He could talk to her about hair and clothing, music and books. It would be a waste of time trying to find anyone else in Bass Beach who could talk about those things.

He ran the palm of his hand over the stubble, then turned to her, grinning. 'Remember when…?' he said, and they fell into their habit of talking about the past, a habit that fitted them like a comfortable pair of shoes.

After a while, Meg said, 'When you sit there with Mr Chatters, what on earth do you talk about?'

Her voice was full of humour. It was a signal to Louis that she wanted a Bass Beach trashing session, but, to Louis, Mr Chatters wasn't a part of the real Bass Beach. 'We talk about The Cowboy Junkies and Terry Pratchett,' he said truthfully.

Meg began to giggle. 'As if. I bet he likes Neil Diamond and Tom Clancy.'

Louis changed the subject. 'One thing he did say, he reckons I've got a neatly shaped head.'

Louis preened before Meg's mirror. She joined him. They struck poses, standing like stick-insect supermodels, sulking, sucking in their cheeks. Louis cheered up. He liked fooling around with Meg.

'How's your navel ring?'

The previous Saturday Meg had gone up to the city and had her navel pierced. She was looking forward to summer, and shocking the locals. She had hoped to shock Carl and Steph into noticing her unhappiness, but they hadn't seemed interested. 'Do your own thing,' was their credo.

Louis watched as she lifted her top away from her stomach and pulled down the waistband of her tights. The skin was less red and swollen-looking than it had been. 'Does it still hurt?'

'Just a bit tender.'

Meg excited Louis. She kept him game. They talked again of their old life. The talking helped, but it also kept their pain in the forefront. They talked about their first day at Bass Beach Secondary College, and that reminded Louis of Tilly Chatterton. 'There's a new kid in my class.'

'I saw her. She's Mr Chatters' niece.'

'Oh. You know.'

'Everyone was talking about her.'

'She's pretty cool,' Louis said offhandedly, trying not to make his interest too plain. 'A nose stud, pierced ears, tattoo.'

'It must freak Mr Chatters out.'

'He didn't seem too concerned.'

'I wonder how long she'll last,' Meg said musingly.

'What do you mean?'

'She got expelled from her last school.'

'Expelled?'

'The kids were talking about it.'

'What did she do?'

'I'll try and find out.'

Louis looked inwards, at his image of Tilly Chatterton casually swinging her legs on her uncle's horsehair sofa and eating her apple; at Tilly solicitously fetching him a glass of water.

Meg nudged him. 'Are you keen on her?'

Louis shrugged.

Meg pushed the subject. 'Why don't you ask her for the Polonaise?'

'Maybe.'

'Go on, ask her. You two would look good together.'

'Think I should?'

'Go for it.'

'What about you?'

'God, I hope no one asks me,' Meg replied, 'and no way am I going to ask anyone. I'm not doing their stupid Polonaise.'

'If you don't, I won't,' Louis said.

Meg rummaged in her jewellery box for a small gold hoop, stepped close to him and held it first against his earlobe and then his upper lip and finally his eyebrow. 'Don't do things just because I do. Be yourself. I think you should ask Tilly. She'll be fun. She'll be good for you.'

SIX

Louis left Meg and went to his room. He hadn't checked on his Terry Pratchett Web site for a couple of days. He booted up his Compaq and logged on. A couple of dozen new hits. Some people gave their first names, others a pseudonym; most said where they were actually from. There were messages congratulating him from Canada, the US, Scotland and Denmark. One new one, just an hour old, was signed *Mathilde*, and he guessed she was French or German. She had some provocative things to say about the first Pratchett novel; he found himself typing in a reply.

There was a knock and Carl came in. He looked tired, his ponytail ragged, his face and forearms streaked with clay. 'Ready, Lou? We'll be in the car.'

They had planned to drive out to the bush block for a couple of hours' work before sundown. There was nothing on the block to look at, only the wreck of a house, a tired fenceline, some scrubby trees and a view of the Bay in the distance. Louis hated going out there. The bush always seemed to close in on him.

He changed rapidly into his old Levis, Nike runners and parka, and joined the others at the car. Steph smiled at him sadly from the front seat. Whatever she'd been discussing with Carl in the shop had left her subdued, for she still wore her work clothes, and she said nothing during the ten-minute ride out to the block. It wasn't until they were bumping along the dirt track that led to the front gate that she spoke:

'I've got some bad news to tell you kids.'

The car slowed. They all turned to her. *We're*

returning to the city, Louis thought. *You little ripper.*

'I've been sacked.'

Louis blinked. He gathered his wits and reached over and touched her shoulder. 'What did you do wrong?'

She shrugged him off crossly and angled around, the seatbelt cutting under her jaw. 'I didn't do anything wrong. I was laid off. They've cut staff by twenty per cent.' She turned away bitterly. 'Redundant to their needs, they said.'

'Oh, Mum,' Meg said, 'twice in twelve months.'

'They're all bastards,' Carl put in. 'They take money away from social welfare and use it to prop up big business.'

'The point is,' Steph wailed, 'where am I going to get another job around here?'

They were silent. The old gums and pines at the road's edge formed a canopy that seemed to press down upon the car and their lives. They came to the white gate posts and the rusting, padlocked gates. Louis got out, unlocked the gates and swung them open for the car. As usual, Carl didn't stop for him but drove through and then out of sight beyond the old house. Louis followed, glancing left across a small paddock toward a rickety windmill on the bank of a leaky dam.

The house was no more than a small weatherboard cabin set on a patch of grass in a grove of ancient fruit trees: quince, pear, apple, plum, persimmon, nectarine, apricot. The late sun slanted through bare licheny branches that were like the bony, reaching fingers of a nightmare creature. Louis shivered. The air was cold. Back in early summer, when he'd first seen the place, the old trees had been hung with fruit and leaves, the sunlight had been soft, the wooden slats of the house warm to the touch.

The previous owners had tried to improve the house. They'd erected the frame for a two-storey extension at one end and attached a pine deck along the northern and western walls. It was Carl's plan to complete the extension, replace the plumbing and wiring, plant a vegetable garden to be irrigated by the windmill, and move the family in, all before Christmas.

Louis had doubts about the windmill. It was

a forlorn-looking thing, like an angel with broken wings.

Then he thought: If Carl's going to have the windmill mended, he'll need an expert to do it, and that expert is Mr Chatters. And if Mr Chatters comes out here, maybe he'll bring Tilly with him. Louis ran to the car, buoyed by the thought, and helped unload.

'Right,' Carl said, 'let's start cutting these weatherboards to size.'

Four thirty. Five o'clock. Five-thirty. They worked, measuring and cutting, a little weighed down by Steph's bad news. As darkness crept over them, the sky to the west turned full mauve, as deep and vibrant as one of Meg's lipstick shades. 'Red sky at night, shepherd's delight,' Carl said.

He's trying to be cheerful for Steph's sake, Louis thought. He'll go too far in a minute and she'll snap at him.

'No rain tomorrow,' Carl went on. 'We can come out here again and nail up these boards.'

Steph finally exploded. 'Oh, bugger your boards.'

'Sweetheart, we—'

'If we've no money coming in, how can we finish the house?'

'We'll manage,' Carl said.

'Every cloud's got a silver lining, that's always been your philosophy.'

'What's wrong with that? Look on the bright side. When the fruit ripens next summer we'll sell it to the local shops. Persimmons, quinces, I bet they can't get ready supplies of them. We'll grow and sell vegetables. You could do some word processing. I'll sell some pots.'

Louis and Meg watched Steph seat herself on the sawhorse, all of her energy gone. She looked defeated in the evening light. 'You all have something you like doing, something you're good at. Me, I've got nothing.'

It was true. Carl had his pots, Meg her drawings, Louis his Terry Pratchett Web site. Steph seemed to have nothing but a deep sad yearning to make something fine with her hands or her head—but what, she didn't know.

'You could write something,' Carl said, packing the saw and his leather carpentry apron into the boot of the car. 'You used to write terrific poetry at school.'

'I haven't got anything to say.'

'You won't know until you try. Or take a painting course. Or help me design pots.'

'Huh,' said Steph humourlessly. 'If you and I worked together we'd be at each other's throats.'

'You'll find something you're good at.'

'I wish we'd never come here.'

Carl looked at her helplessly, his hands collapsed at his sides. 'Oh, please don't say that.'

Louis and Meg, unnoticed by their parents, exchanged a glance full of meaning. Meg winked and grinned. This was the beginning of the end. They'd be back in the city before long.

SEVEN

Louis had learned to time his arrival at school each morning. If too early, he risked encountering Craven and Bird; if too late, he risked detention; and so he always arrived by the first bell.

On Monday morning he noticed a stir of interest as he entered the classroom, an undertow of murmurs and nudges as he wound among the desks and found his seat.

Old Valentine said, 'Bit draughty around the ears this morning, Mr Deane?'

Laughter.

Louis sat and stared ahead expressionlessly. Within himself, he felt elation. They'd marked him out as different. He didn't belong here.

'Looking at that crop of stubble,' Old Valentine said, 'reminds me of the essay topic: "We always hurt the ones we love".'

Uncertain laughter. Old Valentine was always making obscure jokes, his moustache bristling in pleasure at himself.

'Remember, I want to see a draft before the Ball, and a finished essay straight after the September break.'

Later, as the class settled into the rhythms of the day, Louis began to steal looks at Tilly Chatterton. She'd been placed near the front of the room, under the window, two rows over to his right. He wanted her to notice him and he wanted to hear her voice, but she sat still and unresponsive through the morning. She didn't seem to write or read anything; she didn't appear to listen. It was as if she'd shut down, and Louis thought he knew why. The other girls had started a whispering campaign against her, with plenty of exaggerated winks, nudges and secretive huddles, and some of the bolder ones would block her in the aisles and corridors, daring her to complain, while guys like Craven and Bird leered at her, openly commenting on her appearance and speculating about her past. Louis tried to find an opportunity to reassure her, but there were always too many other kids around. I'll try to speak to her at lunchtime, he thought.

But Craven and Bird found him first. They herded him against the wall of the science block, pressing him against the sun-faded and flaking yellow paint of the weatherboards. Louis folded in on himself automatically, chin to chest, shoulders hunched, an arm over his stomach, a hand protecting his groin. It was not that they ever landed hard punches on him, just dozens of quick soft punches that stopped short of hurting him but which, taken together, wore him down, sometimes to tears. Sometimes he wanted to roll into a ball and close his eyes.

He waited for the punches to begin. He waited for the claustrophobia to come swamping through him. Instead, a hand scraped over his bristly head, against the grain. 'Top haircut, Claypot.'

It was Craven, his half-closed eyes blinking at Louis from just centimetres away. Craven's hair brushed Louis' cheek, making his skin crawl. 'Really cool,' Craven said, putting his head to one side assessingly.

Louis looked for the trap. There had to be one. But Craven seemed genuine.

'Thanks,' Louis muttered.

Bird said, 'You mean old Chatters done that?'

Louis couldn't believe that they were talking *to* him, rather than *at* him; couldn't believe they weren't using him as a punching bag. 'Yes.'

'Hard to believe.'

Louis regained some of his confidence. 'He knows what he's doing. And he just did what I asked, no quibbles.'

'Cool.'

As Louis watched them circle him, admiring the haircut, an uncomfortable and confusing realisation settled on him: *It's as though I need their approval. How come? I shouldn't give two hoots what they think of me.*

He said, 'Have you asked anyone for the Polonaise yet?'

'Nup,' Craven said.

'Nup,' Bird said.

'What about you?' Craven said.

Louis replied offhandedly, 'Thought I'd ask Tilly Chatterton.'

Their jaws dropped. 'You must be mad.'

Louis was hurt. 'Why?'

'She's weird.'

'She's all right,' Louis said.

'Sooner you than me, mate,' Craven said, showing his disgust.

'You have to have a partner,' Louis said.

'No you don't.'

Louis looked at Bird, who said, 'I'm not asking anyone.'

'But you're going, aren't you?'

'Yeah, but only so we can sneak out and have a beer and a smoke around the back of the hall,' Bird replied.

Louis scuffed at the dirt with his shoe. He felt Craven's heavy arm go around his shoulders. 'Mate, you can do better than that Chatterton chick. You know what she done, doncha?'

'What?'

'Got caught stealing from the lockers at her last school.'

'Stealing?'

'So I heard,' Craven said. 'Got expelled.'

Bird said, 'She looks like a bit iffy. You can tell.'

And the three of them scanned the schoolyard for Tilly Chatterton, Louis feeling a kind of connection to Craven and Bird. Failing to spot her, they looked inwards, letting her form in their minds: wild hair, pale skin, chewed fingernails, the nose stud, tattoo and pierced ears.

Then Louis remembered Tilly's kindness on Mr Chatters' back porch, her swinging legs and the big green apple in her hand. She wasn't a thief. But he knew better than to contradict Craven and Bird. Besides, for the first time, Craven and Bird were treating him with respect. It's going to be tricky, Louis thought, keeping the respect of Craven and Bird *and* Tilly Chatterton.

He waited for her after school, choosing a street corner where he wouldn't be spotted by anyone. 'Hello.'

She made to pass by him.

'Enjoying the Terry Pratchett?' he called desperately.

She paused, letting him catch up. 'It's all right,' she said, her voice toneless.

'Have you seen the Web site yet?'

She shrugged. 'Might have. Why?'

Louis couldn't work her out. 'Just thought you'd be interested.'

They walked on. He tried something else. 'Your uncle gave me a good cut.'

'I already told you I liked it, Louis.'

'Erm—'

Then she seemed to unbend a little, as though she knew that he wasn't like the others. She turned to face him, swinging her bag. 'I thought Mr Valentine was a bit mean to you.'

'He doesn't scare me,' Louis said.

'Who does?' she asked, narrowing her eyes.

Louis didn't know how to respond. Did she know about Craven and Bird's hold over him? He stammered inanely, 'I'm new here myself.'

'Are you?'

'I hate it,' he admitted.

'You'll get used to it. You can get used to

anything,' Tilly said carelessly, as if to say he shouldn't be a wimp.

He decided to change the subject. The Ball. The Polonaise. He gathered his courage, coughed once, and said, 'I was wondering if—'

But she said immediately, 'Well, see ya!' and ran off.

Louis groaned. He watched her slender legs. After a few metres she turned and smiled and waved, but, somehow, he felt more discouraged than encouraged. He'd blown it.

He continued along High Street, kicking at pebbles. Tilly ran on ahead of him, dodging around a couple of overweight young women who had stopped to gossip, their shopping trolleys—loaded with crisp packets, bottles of soft drink and tubs of icecream—like gaudy roadblocks in her path. When he passed them, they were staring after Tilly, one muttering to the other, 'You know about her, don't you? I wouldn't get too close, you'd catch something off her.'

'Like what?'

'You know, from the needle-sharing and that.'

It was too much for Louis. His frustration

boiled into rage, and he gave them the finger, shouting, 'What would you know, fatso?'

It didn't do him much good. The satisfaction was short-lived, there was clearly a mystery about Tilly, and he was no closer to having her as his partner for the Polonaise.

EIGHT

In the days that followed, Louis felt pushed and pulled by the world. He became obsessed with Tilly, watching her covertly, taking in her solemn, self-contained face, hoping to exchange glances with her, trying to meet her 'accidentally' in the street or a school corridor, yet he was also confused, sometimes wondering if he even liked her very much. She didn't mix, rarely spoke, didn't ruffle any feathers, and did all that was expected of her in the classroom, but no more than that. She was an enigma to

Louis, and it was driving him crazy. Meanwhile the rumours about her intensified. Were they all true? Some of them? None of them? But they can't all be false, can they? Louis thought.

Then there was his haircut. It had been an act of revolt, but scarcely anyone cared, and Craven and Bird had gone back to tormenting him again.

Finally, there was life at home. It was clear that Carl and Steph had no intention of selling up and returning to the city. Steph had begun to look for a new job, Carl continued to fire pots in the kiln, and they all worked on the old house every afternoon before dark. No one but Meg knew Louis' unhappiness.

'When you're feeling down,' she said brightly, 'go shopping. That's what I do.'

'Yeah, right, that should take up about five seconds.'

'Not in Bass Beach, stupid. Take the bus to Fenwick next Saturday.'

Fenwick was a suburb at the south-eastern tip of the city's curve around the bay, forty-five minutes away by bus, and to Louis it was just a larger version of Bass Beach: there were the same seventeen-year-old mothers pushing prams and young guys flipping skateboards. But it did have plenty of arcades and department stores, and he had a hundred and fifty dollars of accumulated pocket money and birthday money in the bank.

'What should I shop for?'

'Clothes.'

Meg was wearing her standard Gothic black today. 'Such as?' Louis asked.

He saw the mischief start up in her. 'How about punk? No? Herbal, some nice itchy hemp cargo pants? Maybe a fleecy check shirt and trackie pants? Or a genuine vinyl jacket?'

'How about moccasins and stretch jeans?'

She punched him on the arm. 'Go for it.'

In the end, he didn't buy clothes but the latest Terry Pratchett, and checked out the CDs in Retro. He passed an hour that way, getting ten per cent off on the book and finding a secondhand copy of a Pink Floyd, and was idling along the software racks in Double Click Computers when he saw Tilly Chatterton.

His body reacted immediately. First his throat seemed to close up, then his heart began to hammer, and finally his palms grew sweaty and a wind roared in his ears. It was the shock of seeing her like that, out of school uniform, in an unexpected place, with strangers, and apparently bubbling over with happiness.

She moved on and he stepped out into the mall for a better look. The strangers with her were kids of her age and they were bumping one another's shoulders and giggling and shouting as they moved down the mall. He began to follow them, keeping well back amongst the drifting knots of shoppers. The cover was good.

Perhaps too good. He lost her.

Louis glanced around wildly. He'd come to the intersection of two long malls, fronted by a donut shop, a jeweller's, a newsagency and a hot-bread kitchen. There: they were buying donuts.

Or her friends were. Where was Tilly?

'Are you following me?'

He jumped and spun around. She grinned, her head on one side. 'I was just . . .' he stammered.

She had her uncle's tact. 'You didn't want to

intrude? It's okay, they're friends from my old school. Come and meet them.'

She dragged him to the donut shop and introduced him. 'This is Ellie, Jess and Rosa. This is Louis.'

They circled him, gazing at him brightly, curiously, a little teasingly. It was not meant cruelly, but he was intimidated.

'They won't bite you,' Tilly said.

They nudged one another. 'But he *is* yummy,' one said, and they all laughed.

Another offered him a donut. 'Here you go, tiger. Get that inside you.'

The third said, 'Can I touch your hair?' and reached up her hand. Louis froze, then reluctantly bowed his head. He felt hands stroking, patting. 'It tickles,' they said. 'It feels nice and soft. Uh oh, sorry, Louis, I had sugar on my fingers.'

Louis' skin burned. He was tongue-tied, and seeing Tilly like this, happy and confident with her friends, told him that the Polonaise idea was absurd. Not in a million years would she be interested in going with him, and he saw himself suddenly through her eyes, just another kid, some young, inoffensive kid, a bit nicer than the rest, but nothing special.

The familiar symptoms of claustrophobia began to creep through him. 'Got to catch the bus,' he shouted desperately, backing away.

He turned and ran. At the corner he stopped to look back. They were killing themselves about something—either about him, or about something else and they'd forgotten him the moment he said goodbye.

NINE

What Louis needed was an act that would shock everyone to their boots—shock his parents into taking him seriously, shock Old Valentine into more than offhand snideness, shock Tilly into looking at him with new eyes, and show Craven and Bird that he had more nerve than they did.

The following Saturday morning he took the train up to the city. As far as anyone knew, he was meeting his old city friends to see the new James Bond film. Instead, they went straight to Metallica, where Louis spent forty dollars on an ear stud and an eyebrow ring, and two of his friends were fitted with nose studs. The friends were self-conscious afterwards, holding their hands over their red and swollen noses, while Louis' earlobe and eyebrow throbbed, but the pain made them feel good—risky, at the edge of things rather than back in the pack. After that, Louis spent his last seventy dollars on a new computer game called Powerslide.

'Hey, neat,' Meg said, when he walked in the door that evening.

He went into the sitting room. Steph looked up from her book. 'That looks a bit sore, dear. Put some cream on it.'

Carl looked around from the football replay. 'How much?'

Louis said defiantly, 'Forty dollars.'

'Suits you. Watch out when you dry yourself after a shower, though.'

Didn't anything stir Carl and Steph? Louis wanted a reaction from them, not this hippy tolerance and caring crap. 'I have to keep the rings in for six weeks until the holes heal,' he said.

'Uh huh.'

Louis shut himself in his room, booted up the

Compaq, and didn't emerge until Monday morning. Plenty of hits at his Web site, from all over the world. Several messages from Mathilde in Europe.

He was deliberately late getting to school. He walked calmly past Old Valentine, sat down, and relished the moment when the other kids saw his new rings. He saw them huddling, leaning across the aisles to one another, pointing, whispering, and it felt good.

Old Valentine still hadn't spotted the rings. 'Nice of you to grace us with your presence, Mr Deane.'

Louis had never felt so bold before. 'You're welcome, sir.'

Any moment now... Yes! Old Valentine gaped. 'What's that on your face?'

Louis' hand flashed to his eyebrow. 'Just a ring, sir.'

'Just a ring, sir. Let's have a look at it. Stand up, come out here where we can all see you.'

Louis climbed slowly out of his seat and shuffled to the front of the room.

'Turn around. Now, peasants, we are privileged to have among us today a genuine sideshow freak. Normally you'd have to go to the showgrounds and pay good money to point and stare, but today we can do that for free.'

Louis felt something hard push at his back. Old Valentine was poking him with a ruler. The cruel voice continued: 'I wonder if this specimen can talk? Got something to say to us, freak?'

Louis said nothing. He stared out above their heads. He didn't want to see their avid faces. But then his gaze was drawn to Tilly Chatterton. She wasn't sharing in the mob feeling. He saw her eyes flicker, acknowledging him.

Another sharp prod. 'Perhaps you're not aware of it, Chuckles, but we have a dress code in this school, a uniform policy. It doesn't allow for weird body adornment.'

Louis couldn't help himself. He turned and said, 'You mean like your moustache, sir? Will you have to shave it off now?'

The class roared. Old Valentine's moustache was a sparse gingery growth that reached down on each side of his mouth like a dying house plant. When he grinned, or bared his teeth in anger, individual hairs popped free—like short, cropped pubes, Louis thought, as he saw it happen now.

'You little beggar,' Old Valentine said, and five minutes later Louis found himself explaining his conduct to the principal.

'You may wear your earring—I have given up trying to ban them—so long as it's discreet,' the principal said finally. 'But I don't expect to see you wearing an eyebrow ring again, is that clear?'

Louis decided to enjoy himself a little. 'But the hole will close up, sir.'

'What part of my instruction didn't you understand, mister? You-are-not-to-wear-an-eyebrow-ring-at-this-school, is that clear?'

'Yes, sir. Sir, what if I put a plaster over it during school hours so it won't be obvious?'

'You're trying my patience, Mr Deane. You're asking for a suspension.'

Five minutes later, Louis was back in the classroom, minus the eyebrow ring—it was that, or go home and explain to the oldies why he'd been banned from attending Bass Beach Secondary College forever.

At the bike rack later Craven said, 'Should of seen Old Valentine's face.'

'Like he'd pooped his pants,' Bird agreed.

Louis basked in their approval. Craven and Bird spent most of their lives being tongue-lashed by Old Valentine. They were glad to see it happening to Louis for a change, and excited to see Louis strike back.

They demanded to see his pierced skin. There wasn't much to see, just two small reddish dampish puncture wounds at the corner of his eyebrow, but both boys were consumed with curiosity.

'Did it hurt?'

'Not much. It's over quickly.'

'Much blood?'

'No.'

It worked, Louis thought. They *admire* me. I've had the nerve to do things they want to do but can't.

They stayed close to Louis all that week. They asked for his help with their homework, told him dirty jokes, showed him shortcuts through the town, took him smoking at the jetty, coached him in how to shoplift at the supermarket. In return he showed them his Web site and let them reply to Mathilde and the others—not that Craven and Bird had much to say and they didn't get Terry Pratchett's humour at all.

He seemed to fascinate them. It was as if the balance had been tipped permanently this time. They wouldn't be going back to their old ways with him.

It was an odd relationship. Craven and Bird admired him, protected him, called him their friend, yet there was nothing about their tastes and attitudes that he shared. But he didn't mind: he felt safe with them, could be himself at last, and he wore their approval like a cloak.

That left Tilly Chatterton. Louis coasted through the next few days, his spirits high. He didn't anticipate any problems: he'd seen her sympathetic glances during Old Valentine's tirade.

It wasn't until Friday that he had a chance to seek her out. He'd just finished his Desktop Publishing elective, she her Drama elective, and he tracked her down to the dark corridor outside the dressing rooms behind the stage of the performing arts centre.

She was not alone.

'Come on baby, light my fire,' a male voice said.

'Hey, baby, float my boat,' said another.

They were ugly, inflamed voices. Louis kept well back, concealed by the shadows, and poked his head around the edge of a bulky filing cabinet marked 'costumes'.

There were about eight of them and they had Tilly's back to the wall opposite the girls' dressing room. She wore a short, Roman-style tunic, and two Year 10 kids, who always had girls hanging around them, were attempting to lift the hem with a cardboard Centurion's sword while the girls looked on and sniggered. Tilly shrank away from them, bunching the tunic around her thighs with both hands. She didn't say a word.

'Come on, Cleopatra, show us what you've got.'

'Strip, strip, strip,' the girls chanted, clapping their hands. They were the best looking and most popular girls in the school. It's not true that bullies are always the ugly outcasts, Louis thought.

The corridor was dusty and airless. He wanted to sneeze. And a couple of the Drama girls were still in the process of changing from their Roman costumes. While the others taunted Tilly, they looked on eagerly from the dressing room, chewing gum, shouting and spraying themselves with deodorant and body-spray on to and under their street clothes. The fumes rolled thickly down the corridor and Louis wanted to gag.

'Look, don't be a spoilsport, Tilly.'

Louis tried to breathe shallowly.

'Can't fool us, Tilly,' one of the girls said. 'We know all about you.'

'Oi! What's going on here?'

It was the principal, coming along the corridor from the opposite direction.

Louis slipped away.

As he went, he thought: Lucky the principal came in time. He thought: Lucky I didn't have to get involved. And he thought: But *would* I have got involved?

He didn't derive any comfort from the answer.

TEN

He'd been gutless. No one else knew, but he knew, and that was enough. Louis was reminded of something that Mr Chatters had once said: 'Set high standards for yourself'. Funny how you ignore it, resent it, when an adult says stuff like that, he thought, then one of their sayings turns around and bites you on the bum.

He'd set a pretty low standard for himself, letting Tilly be bullied.

So, better do something about it.

Mr Chatters was the key.

Louis found Mr Chatters in his driveway, staring mournfully at the Austin truck. 'Some dipstick's nicked my bonnet ornament,' he said.

Louis peered at the nose of the faded red bonnet. The flying *A* had been wrenched out, leaving two bruised, rusty holes in the metal.

'I tell you, Lou, if I ever find who did it, I'll nail his hide to the wall.'

Louis nodded in commiseration. 'It's a shame.'

'You after a haircut?'

'It's a bit fluffy looking.'

Mr Chatters laughed and clapped him across the shoulders. 'Like bum fluff?'

Louis went red.

Pink Floyd's 'The Wall' was playing on the salon radio. Louis said, 'That's a coincidence—I bought this CD the other day.'

The clippers buzzed about his neck. 'Did you?'

Louis had been wondering how to broach the subject of Tilly. Pink Floyd was the hook he needed. 'In Fenwick. I saw Tilly there.'

'Did you?'

'She was with some friends.'

With a trace of bitterness, Mr Chatters said,

'Poor kid, has to travel miles to be among friends.'

'Like me,' Louis said hotly. 'I have to go up to the city.'

'Not like you at all, Louis. You haven't been through what she's going through.'

Louis fell silent at that. He wanted to know more about Tilly. He wanted to know what she thought of him. He also wanted to steer the conversation on to the subject of the Polonaise, his availability as a partner for Tilly, and his suitability as a friend. In fact, Louis wanted Mr Chatters to engineer the whole thing and get him together with Tilly.

It would never happen. Now that he'd set his aims out so clearly in his head, he saw how far-fetched they were.

Yet he had to try. He cleared his throat. 'I'll have to line up a partner for the Polonaise pretty soon.'

Instead of taking the bait, Mr Chatters picked up the scissors and clacked them furiously. 'Know what I did this morning? Spent the whole flaming time on the blower, ringing around wreckers' yards. They said the only place

I'd find a replacement bonnet ornament for a truck that old was England. Bloody kids, I swear.'

'I'll keep an eye open for it,' Louis said, thinking that he wouldn't have to look far. Start with the kids in Year 8.

The scissors fell silent. 'I hope you're not intending to dob anyone in, Louis. No one likes a sneak.'

That was unfair. Louis stammered, 'I mean—'

But Mr Chatters had a gift for turning bad situations around. 'I think you mean,' he interrupted kindly, 'that you'd gently but firmly inform whoever took my bonnet ornament that I'd appreciate its return, no questions asked, am I right?'

'Yes,' Louis said, his voice shaky with relief.

But he'd lost his nerve now. He felt small and immature, and no match for Tilly Chatterton or her uncle.

Mr Chatters stooped to peer at his face. 'Your eyebrow looks a bit sore. Pimple?'

Louis couldn't wait to get out of there.

He banged through the gate, straight into a

knot of Year 9 girls slouching home along Whiting Street, chewing gum and smoking.

'Girls, look, it's that sex god, Louis Deane.'

'Whatcha doin here, Looee, Looee?'

'He's waiting for that Chatterton bitch.'

'He'll have to wait in line behind all the other guys, ha ha.'

Louis felt their poison in his veins. He could see Tilly at the end of the street, far behind, as if to avoid overtaking them. 'Piss off,' he said.

'Oooh, language, young man.'

When they had moved on, he headed along Whiting Street, intending to pass Tilly with a short 'hi', nothing more, but she stopped him.

'Louis, can I ask you something?'

'Er, okay.'

She blushed. She looked away. She struggled to find the words. Finally, she said, 'Will you please be my partner for the Polonaise?'

The world seemed to stand still.

She looked at him. 'Please?'

Her mouth opened a little. Something glinted in there. She had a stud in her tongue. You'd scarcely notice it normally.

Louis thought: She's too far out for me.

The wind rushed in his ears. He found himself saying, 'Sorry, already got a partner, sorry.'

ELEVEN

Now what was he going to do?

He spent the weekend feeling paralysed. He tried to throw himself into homework, Terry Pratchett, anything at all, but nothing helped.

On Monday morning, the rough drafts of their essays were collected. Louis wanted to hide; five minutes later, he heard Old Valentine say, 'Louis Deane, what do you call this?'

Louis looked up and recognised his quarter page of handwriting flapping in Old Valentine's hand. 'My essay, sir.'

The voice dripped with sarcasm. 'Your essay. Do you know what an essay is? It presents a reasoned argument about a specific topic. It has a beginning, a middle and an end. It examines a proposition, giving reasons for and against, and comes to a balanced conclusion. *This*,' Old Valentine sneered, 'is not an essay.'

Louis heard bored laughter from a couple of the others. They weren't laughing at Louis in particular—Old Valentine was always sounding off about things like essays. But was Tilly laughing with them? She'd have the right to.

Old Valentine was warming up. With relish he read aloud what Louis had written:

'"We always hurt the ones we love. Discuss." Well, at least you got the topic right.'

More laughter.

'"It's not true that we always hurt the ones we love,"' Old Valentine read. '"We hurt some but not others. We also hurt those we don't love. Sometimes we are too close to the person and don't realise we are hurting them. There are different ways of hurting someone, like neglect, physical force and lying to them. Worst of all is when we make the person do what they don't want to do."'

When he'd written those last two sentences, Louis had been thinking first of Tilly's disappointed face and then of the way he and Meg had been forced by Carl and Steph to move to Bass Beach against their will. That had been at eight o'clock last night, school the next morning, the rough draft due first thing, but although he knew he was expected to write three or four pages, he'd been too miserable to continue, and so he'd handed the draft in as it was.

'You peasant,' Old Valentine said now. 'Where's the rest?'

But Louis wasn't listening. There was to be Polonaise practice on the tennis courts after lunch, with further practice sessions all week, and a final practice in the shire hall itself on Friday morning, before the Ball that night. Louis figured that he had just one hundred and eight hours in which to find a partner—fewer, if he accounted for sleeping, eating, schoolwork, homework, restoring the house on the bush block and watching TV. Maybe—he did some rapid calculations in his head—as little as ten or twenty hours.

He swallowed. His mouth was dry. He felt a surge of panic. Old Valentine continued to rant and rave, but was scarcely real to Louis: no more than one of those open-mouthed, swivel-necking clowns you try to throw balls into at the show.

A hand waved in front of Louis. 'Hello? Anybody in there?'

Louis blinked. 'Sorry, sir.'

'You're going to be sorry if I don't get a better essay than this from you after the September break. Try again. There are clearly some ideas lurking in this rubbish, but more depth next time, more substance, understand?'

'Yes, sir.'

Louis returned to his seat. He avoided looking at Tilly. All weekend he'd been haunted by her face. There had been hope in it when she approached him last Friday—hope, courage and shy affection—but he'd destroyed it with a simple lie. He could still picture the way her face had altered, collapsing into pain, disappointment and embarrassment, still see her spinning around and fleeing home without a word.

Straight home to tell Mr Chatters?

Could he retrieve the situation? He was fond of her, wasn't he? He didn't really believe all of the stories about her, did he? He was big enough to ignore Craven and the others, surely?

He could tell her sorry, he'd made a mistake, he'd be delighted to be her partner.

No. She would have too much pride to accept that. Besides, it hadn't been a simple lie at all. She'd want to know why he was suddenly free to partner her. She'd want to know what had happened to his first 'partner'.

Perhaps he could say this imaginary partner had the flu?

No. She'd try to work out who it was.

Perhaps he could go to the Ball *without* a partner. Then he could ask Tilly to be his partner, say his own partner had fallen ill at the last minute.

But what if someone else asked her in the meantime?

He'd look like an idiot then.

Perhaps he could feign illness and stay home.

But he badly wanted to go. Sure, the Polonaise sounded daggy, but the excitement surrounding it was infectious.

As Louis saw it, he had no choice but to find a partner for the Polonaise quickly, before the first practice session, and on the night itself have all of the other dances with Tilly. After all, he hadn't told her he wouldn't or couldn't *dance* with her on the night, just that he couldn't partner her for the Polonaise.

At the lesson change, he approached Anna Mercurio. 'Would you be my partner for the Polonaise?'

'Sorry, I've got someone.'

During morning recess he walked the yard and sidled up to Jo Solberg. 'I want to ask if you could be my partner for the Polonaise, please.'

'Sorry. Can't.'

At lunchtime he roamed between the library, the basketball court and the lunchroom. Three times he mumbled the words: 'Would you please be my partner for the Polonaise?' and heard the three replies with a sinking heart:

'Sorry.'

'No way.'

'Can't. Sorry.'

He was desperate now. Even Craven had a partner. After lunch, when the whole school assembled for Polonaise practice, Louis scanned the crowd of kids. No sign of Tilly. She always went home for lunch, so maybe she was late. Or maybe she intended to miss Polonaise practice and the Ball itself? Yes, that was it. Louis felt that he'd been let off the hook.

Unfortunately he was told to partner Bird.

'Just for now,' the principal said irritably. 'By Friday evening I expect both of you boys to have partners.'

Trying hard to ignore the jibes of the other kids, Louis got into position. Bird was mortified. When the music began, and the lines moved, Louis felt as if he were partnering a buffalo. Bird was too clumsy, too hefty, too heavy on his feet. He also ponged. Kids would play football and netball at lunchtime, rain or shine, and come back smelling of sweaty socks, wet wool, unwashed bodies and ladled-on deodorant. Sometimes the teachers would head for an open window and teach from there. But Louis decided to make the best of it, and threw himself into the dance. It was satisfying being part of a long, weaving, splitting-and-reforming snake.

Then, in the midst of the stumbles and collisions, the principal's shouts and the scrape of confused feet, the scratchy music and Bird's sweaty gasps, he found himself face to face with Tilly Chatterton.

She'd arrived unnoticed by Louis, and been partnered with Old Valentine, who was beaming like a clown and humming to himself. When she saw who Louis' partner was, she looked stunned. As Louis watched, her eyes filled with pain. She knows I lied, he thought. He tried to speak. His mouth opened. His voice choked on a word that might have been *Tilly*, or *sorry*, or *please*, but by then Old Valentine had turned her away with a graceful dip and flourish, and she was gone from Louis' sight.

TWELVE

Tilly didn't appear at school on Tuesday.

Or Wednesday.

The rumours crept like stains through Year 8.

'She's been arrested.'

'She's had an overdose.'

'I saw her in the Fenwick mall with a gang of bikies.'

'She's been expelled.'

But Louis knew better. She was hiding at home because he'd hurt her.

After school that Wednesday afternoon, he found Steph beaming in her favourite chair. 'Guess what?' she said.

Louis knew instinctively. He seemed to have grown an inbuilt radar that detected and attracted bad news of all kinds. 'You've got a job,' he said sulkily, 'meaning we're stuck in this hole forever.'

Steph stared at him for some time. Then she said quietly, 'Nice to see you so happy for me, Louis.'

Louis blushed. Steph was almost never sarcastic, so he must have crossed the line. 'Sorry.'

'Don't you want to know about the job?'

'I suppose.'

'Such enthusiasm. Well, Mr Smartarse, it's a mail run.'

Louis looked at her in astonishment. 'A mail run?'

'I start next Monday, officially, but tomorrow and Friday I go out with the current mail contractor.'

'Where?'

She fetched a map of the Peninsula and

showed him a grid of interlocking roads inland of Bass Beach. 'It'll be perfect,' she said. 'I start early and finish about midday, leaving the afternoons free for writing.'

Louis pictured the backroads of the district, the strange, mutating mailboxes at every driveway entrance—huge, fat milk cans, wooden crates, dinky hardware store boxes too small for the average letter, fuel cans with half-moons cut out of the tops of them. He could see his mother getting lost or driving through a fence or into a creek or hitting a wandering cow somewhere.

'Great,' he said woodenly, and went in search of Meg. She'd cheer him up.

In fact, why not ask *her* to partner him on Friday night? That would solve everything.

She was staring at herself in her mirror. 'Meg—'

She spun around. She was sparkling with happiness. 'Hi. Did Mum tell you her good news?'

'What's good about it? Makes it harder for us to leave now.'

Meg gestured. 'Oh, we were dreaming, Louis.

We're here to stay. Anyway, once you've finished Year 12 you can leave.'

'Traitor,' he retorted.

She was in a bubbly mood. 'Guess what!'

'What?'

'I've been asked for the Polonaise!'

Louis could only stare at her. He found his voice. 'But you said—'

'I know, I know, but this amazing guy in Year 12 asked me today and I just said yes.'

She seemed to lift off the ground. Louis couldn't bear it. He turned away, muttering, 'You bitch.'

Meg's elation vanished. Her fingers clamped around his upper arm and she shook him, saying, 'Don't you *ever* talk to me like that.'

'Who asked you?'

'Andy Craven.'

Craven's older brother. He was Craven's opposite —tall, athletic, reasonably good-looking. He was also cool, which meant that he stood around scowling and wasn't prepared to string more than two words together at a time. He was more like a city kid than a Bass Beach kid, so Louis could see why Meg liked him. He said miserably, 'But I haven't got anyone to be my partner now.'

'You were going to ask *me*?'

'Yes.'

'What's going on? I thought you were going to ask Tilly, but at Monday's practice she was with Mr Valentine and you with that Bird idiot, and yesterday and today I didn't see her at all. Time's running out.'

Louis groaned, 'I know.'

'What's wrong?'

He told her what he'd done. 'So,' he said in conclusion, 'she must be upset with me.'

Meg was appalled. *'Louis!'*

He flinched. 'Don't yell.'

'You deserve it. How would you feel if you'd asked her and she'd said she had a partner, then later you learnt she'd been lying? It would seem like deliberate cruelty.'

'Don't.'

'A real slap in the face.'

Louis shouted, 'I know that! You don't have to tell me! But what am I going to do, that's what I want to know?'

Meg stared hard at him. 'You need to apologise, for a start.'

Louis looked away. He couldn't meet her eye. Apologise? That was like climbing Mount Everest. It seemed impossible.

Meg shook him. 'Louis, let's get something straight. Do you *want* her to be your partner?'

'I don't know.'

'You seemed keen on her a few days ago.'

Louis muttered, 'She's got a stud in her tongue.'

That stopped Meg for a moment. 'Really? Cool.'

'Plus,' Louis said, 'all those things she's done.'

'Yeah, right,' Meg said. 'If someone in this town tells you something, then it must be true. Carl and Steph tried to con us that country towns are tolerant and friendly, but this one's not. Haven't people got better things to do?'

She pushed Louis away. 'Besides, I thought you liked Tilly because she was different. She was going to be your soul mate—both of you outsiders, both liking to look different from everyone else.'

Louis listened to that term in his head: *soul mate*. He liked the sound and sense of it.

'So, how about it?' Meg demanded.

'What?'

'An apology, you moron.'

'How?'

'Easy,' Meg said. 'Just go around there and say you're sorry.'

Louis had been thinking about having one final trim before the Ball. He could also lend her the Terry Pratchett he'd bought in Fenwick.

'But what do I say? How can I make it sound all right?'

Meg was plucking at her hair and her clothes, which she always did when she was irritable or frustrated. 'I don't know, a little white lie. Tell her you were too shy, tell her your partner changed her mind. Or simply tell her the *truth*, that you shouldn't have listened to the rumours. Tell her you *like* her—I bet that's what she badly wants to hear right now.'

She watched him then, waiting for a response. 'Well? Do you think you can do that?'

'What about the Polonaise?'

'Ask her. Be gracious about it. Tell her you

realise she might have a partner by now, and that you understand why she wouldn't *want* to partner you, but if she's still interested, you'd be honoured to partner her.'

Louis looked away gloomily. It all sounded too hard.

THIRTEEN

But at five o'clock he found himself walking back along High Street to Whiting Street. Whiting Street—living in Bass Beach was like living in a fish and chip shop, he thought. Flounder Street. Flake Terrace. Salt and Vinegar Crescent. It had been raining all week. There were muddy craters in the side streets. A wintry damp wind lashed his cheeks and bare ears and neck. Maybe he was mad to have a haircut.

He ducked under the dripping trees and into Mr Chatters' salon. He almost pitched forward through the door: the old wooden step was slick and green with moisture.

The salon was deserted. Louis moved his rear into a comfortable position on the horsehair sofa and hunted through the pile of magazines. The radio was playing softly, so that he wasn't at first aware of a raised voice inside the house itself. He tiptoed to the door, and realised that he was listening to one side of a telephone conversation.

'Try the homeless shelters, love.'

Pause.

'Talk to the police again.'

Pause.

'Ask at her old school.'

Pause.

'I realise that, Jess.'

Jess. He's talking to Mrs Chatters, Louis thought. What was going on?

'All right. Yes, I'll be here, love. Fine. Bye, bye.'

Louis continued to listen. The house had fallen silent again. After a while, Mr Chatters wandered out from the kitchen. He didn't seem to register that Louis was waiting for a haircut, but sat in his barber's chair and gazed at the sodden garden, which was darkening now as the cloud-obscured sun slipped toward the horizon.

'Mr Chatterton?'

Mr Chatters glanced wonderingly around at Louis. 'Oh, it's you.'

'Can I have a haircut, please?'

Mr Chatters' face twisted. 'Can I have a haircut, please? Can I have a haircut, please? Butter wouldn't melt in your mouth, would it, eh?'

Louis swallowed. He began to leave.

Mr Chatters got out of his chair. 'Where are you going? Come on, sit down.'

Louis approached the chair reluctantly.

'Come on, I won't bite. Though I ought to. How do you want it cut?'

'Like the last time.'

Mr Chatters switched on the electric razor. 'You're a little shit, do you know that?'

Louis felt himself go hot with shame. *Tilly's told him what I did to her.*

But Mr Chatters went on: 'Oh, not you, maybe. She actually said she liked you, you were different, but the other kids at that school of yours—in fact, the whole flaming town—have given her nothing but a hard time.'

'Tilly?'

'Who the hell do you think I'm talking about?' Mr Chatters snarled, 'Elle Macpherson? Of course I mean Tilly.'

Louis said nothing.

Mr Chatters made long, precise sweeps of the razor through Louis' stubble. 'That poor kid's out there somewhere and we don't know where she is. The wife's gone up to town to try and find her. We've phoned everywhere we can think of...'

'What happened?'

'What happened? Haven't you been paying attention? She ran away Monday night.'

Monday, thought Louis. So it *was* my fault. He found himself saying foolishly, 'Where did she go?'

'Are you thick or something? If I knew where she'd gone I'd go and fetch her back, now wouldn't I?'

Louis wanted to cry. He hadn't known he could cause so much hurt.

'The wife and I are going out of our minds

with worry. What if she's hitchhiking and some pervert picks her up? What will she do for money? What if she ends up in Kings Cross?'

The world turned risky and unpredictable in Louis' head. If something bad happens to her, he thought, I will kill myself. Just the fact of his causing her enough pain to run away made him the worst person he knew.

'This town and the morons at that school of yours have had it in for my niece from the start. She never stood a chance.'

Louis waited. He didn't trust himself to speak.

'She told me what people were saying. As if she'd ever take drugs! As if she'd ever offer herself around! You're all sick.'

Louis found his voice. 'We heard—'

'Well you heard wrong. I don't like to think ill of her mum and dad, but they weren't good parents. They let her bring herself up. Eventually things caught up with them and now they're paying the penalty, and that's why Tilly came here to stay with us.'

Louis began to turn his head.

'Keep still. Nearly done.'

Just as Mr Chatters finished, the phone rang inside the house. He rushed away, leaving Louis cloaked in the hair-spiked sheet. Louis waited. Mr Chatters' words were pitched too low to be understood this time.

After a while, Louis shrugged off the sheet, shook it, placed his five dollars on the chair, and began to leave.

Then he remembered the Terry Pratchett in the pocket of his coat. He scribbled in it with the hairy ballpoint pen that Mr Chatters kept with his combs and clippers: *To Tilly. I hope you like this book. From your friend, Louis Deane.*

Louis rolled his neck and shoulders as he walked home. There were hairs inside his collar like needles, tormenting him.

FOURTEEN

It was Friday evening, an hour before they were due at the shire hall, and Louis could feel the old badness creeping through him. They'd all let him down. First Meg, twittering on the phone to a friend about the Ball—What dress? What shoes? How are you doing your hair?—as she sat with towels around her head and her body, painting her toenails. Meg had turned a hundred and eighty degrees, it seemed to Louis. He hadn't known she'd even made a friend at the school; first he'd heard of it. And how had

Craven's older brother screwed up the courage to ask her? And why had she said yes? Just at that moment, Louis hated her.

And Steph and Carl. They were excited, too, Carl in a decent modern jacket he'd bought in Recycle, with a black shirt, weird tie and Levis, Steph in a short black cocktail dress, black tights and her hair tumbling down around her shoulders.

Louis went to his room and flung himself across the bed. He felt lost. He couldn't go forward, he couldn't go back. Five-thirty, six, six-thirty, seven. Still he hadn't showered, changed, or decided what he'd wear.

'*Louis*,' Meg said, opening his door. 'We have to leave soon.'

'Not going.'

'Don't be stupid.' She opened his wardrobe and clacked through the clothes on his hangers. 'Haven't got much, have you?'

'So, I'm not going.'

'We'll improvise,' she said. She took out his black stovepipe jeans and a black shirt. 'You need something over it.'

'Haven't got anything.'

'I've got something. Wait here.'

She was back a minute later with her maroon silk waistcoat. 'Tie?'

'Haven't got one,' he muttered.

'I wish you'd cheer up. Come on, get your act together.'

'I could wear your dunny ring.'

'Too daggy for a ball. Wait here.'

She returned with a silver and turquoise Navaho Indian bolo on a leather thong. She folded the thong under his collar, tightened the clasp, stood back critically. 'Fantastic.'

He examined his reflection in the mirror. The black suited him. He liked the contrasting maroon and turquoise. He knew he'd look different from all of the other kids, and liked that idea. That's what he was about, being different. He peered closer. Good. No pimples, or not much evidence of them.

'Shoes?'

Louis was feeling warm toward Meg again. He pulled out his Doc Martens. 'These.'

Meg looked doubtfully at the scuffed black leather and yellow stitching. 'They *look* cool, but they won't be good to dance in.'

'Why?'

'Too much grip.'

Louis thought that given the kind of dancing he intended to do, wild stuff to shake everyone up, he'd *need* plenty of grip. 'I haven't got any other shoes,' he said, 'except the Nikes.'

They looked at his Nikes: dirt, grease, cracks, muddy frayed laces, a trace of tomato sauce. Meg said, 'The boots for sure.'

Louis pulled on the Doc Martens. He spat on the toe and rubbed at a spot with his handkerchief.

'How charming,' Meg said.

He ignored her. He could feel the force of her scrutiny. Her tactic was to wait him out. She'd stand there and stare at him until he could no longer bear it. He gave up finally, and looked back at her. 'Well, what?'

'As if you couldn't guess.'

He said nothing.

'*Tilly*, you moron,' Meg said. 'Any news?'

'No.'

'I've been listening to the radio and reading the papers.'

So had Louis. He was waiting for some terrible headline: Human Remains Found.

Meg suddenly reached out with both hands and pulled him hard against her waist. 'Don't worry. She'll turn up somewhere.'

'Plenty don't,' Louis said. 'Plenty are never seen again.'

And in this instance it was all his fault.

Meg released him. He felt cold and bereft, his body needing her arms around him again. Whose arms would he feel during the Polonaise? Surely not that idiot, Bird, the teachers couldn't be that cruel.

Who, then?

FIFTEEN

His spirits lifted when he stepped through the doors of the shire hall. The decorations, the music, the dresses, the smiles, the hunger for affection and excitement combined to turn his gloominess away.

Even Bird was affected. His eyes like bright buttons, he nudged Louis at one point and said, 'Look at what's-her-face.'

He meant Ms Tomei, who taught Year 12 Chemistry. Everyone knew that she had a sharp and unforgiving tongue, and spent a lot on clothes, but her love life was a mystery. Tonight she was spinning around the dance floor with a tall, slender, smiling man, and couldn't take her eyes away from his face. The girls were watching her covertly, enviously. So was Bird, as though he felt a stir of something inside himself, a recognition that the world was more complex than he'd imagined, and had more to offer.

Louis gazed up at the walls and ceiling: balloons, banners, streamers. The lighting was dim. He looked down. The vast, waxy, hardwood floor was patterned with drifts of sawdust. As he watched, Ms Tomei spun past, her arm locked horizontally with her boyfriend's, almost as if they were skating on ice. Louis felt exhilarated.

'Music's not bad,' Bird said.

The Mud Flats, from the next town around from Bass Beach, were grouped on the stage at the back of the hall, their tuxedos and white shirts dazzling under the spotlights. They slipped easily from a soft waltz to a thumping rap. Louis watched the dancers laugh and disengage and try the new step. Then it was a tango. Louis' feet itched to dance.

Bird nudged him. 'There's your oldies.'

Carl and Steph whizzed past. Their heads were tipped back. They were laughing, elated.

Then came other parents, including Bird's, and people Louis had never seen before, and Old Valentine and his wife, then the principal, and Ms Tomei again, and twice Meg twirled by, grinning and wrinkling her nose at him.

The music stopped. Louis saw the principal climb up on to the stage and lean into the microphone. 'Ladies and gentlemen, your attention please. It's time for the highlight of the evening, the Polonaise. Students, kindly take your places.'

The adults melted away from the dance floor to line the walls and group in the corners. The teachers—all, except for Old Valentine, grinning their heads off—began to coax and shepherd the kids into position. Louis found himself saying, 'Sir, I haven't got a partner.'

Old Valentine looked at him irritably. 'Well, whose fault is that, mister?'

Bird said, 'I haven't got one either, sir.'

Louis kicked Bird in the shins. 'Ow,' Bird said. 'What did you do that for?'

Louis hissed, 'Do you want to be partnered with me?'

'No.'

'So shut up and stop drawing attention to us.'

Old Valentine hadn't heard the exchange. There was something different about him. Then Louis realised—he'd shaved off his moustache. He didn't look better for it, just marginally different. Louis watched him scanning the room, trying to suck the ends of his invisible whiskers. He saw his face light up. 'Ah, there you are, sweetheart. I've a little favour to ask.'

Thirty seconds later, Bird found himself partnered with Mrs Valentine.

That left Louis without a partner. He began to edge away, intending to hide amongst the parents, but a hand grabbed his arm, and he found himself looking into the sparkling friendly teeth and smiling eyes of Ms Tomei. He could smell her—soap and shampoo—and hear her: 'Louis, may I have the pleasure of this dance?'

Louis felt hot, and stupid, and very pleased with himself. All of his cares vanished.

They only returned when there was a

commotion at the door and Mr Chatters entered, with Tilly on his arm. He snarled at Old Valentine, who was trying to stop him from joining the line of waiting dancers, 'Like it or lump it, pal, we're here to stay.'

SIXTEEN

Louis saw the shock register in everyone's faces. There were snorts, giggles, some nudging and winking amongst the kids and their parents. In response, Mr Chatters swung his big head about, directing his hard stare around the hall. He seemed to be saying, 'Got a problem, pal?'

Meanwhile Tilly waited at his side. She was very still and pale, gazing ahead, solitary and defiant. Louis willed her to look across at him, but her eyes never wavered.

Then the music started, slow and measured,

and the line began to move. Louis tried not to think about Tilly. He concentrated on not making a fool of himself with Ms Tomei. He began to enjoy himself. Ms Tomei's firm hand was in his, her flank banged against him, her hair swung about her shoulders, and her feet, quick and effortless, directed him as the lines of dancers parted and altered direction and reformed again up and down the hall. Her concentration on him was forceful and absolute: she wanted to know all about him, asking questions, making observations, coaxing opinions out of him. And, all the while, there was the beat of the music, the swishing dresses, the shoe-scrape undercurrent, and the proud, cheesy grins of the onlooking parents.

Louis was in a daze when it finished. He thanked Ms Tomei and headed for the back corner. Bird found him and said, 'Half your luck.'

Louis grinned. 'How was Mrs Valentine?'

'Didn't say a word to me, stuck-up bitch. She kept her distance and kept looking down at my feet for some reason.'

Louis laughed.

'How about Tilly and Old Chatters?' Bird said, nudging Louis with his elbow. 'My mum reckoned there was something going on there. Looks like she was right.'

Louis recoiled from Bird. Bird made him feel grubby. He scanned the room. There, in the other corner, Mr Chatters was yarning with Carl. Louis looked around again. This time he found Mrs Chatters, through the archway to the supper room, serving cups of tea to some of the parents.

But where was Tilly?

Craven joined them. He was rubbing his shins. 'My bitch kicked me.'

Bird laughed.

Louis ignored them. He kept searching the room.

'Who're you looking for?'

Bird sniggered. 'He's looking for Tilly Chatterton.'

'He won't find her,' Craven said. He nudged Bird. 'Not unless he looks in the carpark.'

They began to shove each other, snorting with laughter.

'What's so funny?'

'You don't know what she's up to, do you?' Craven said. 'You haven't a clue, poor bastard.'

Louis clenched his fists. 'Tell me.'

'She's waiting outside. She's charging five dollars.' He pointed. 'I heard them talking about it.'

Louis followed Craven's thick finger. Brett Matthews, Justin Kolodny, Eddie Elliott, a couple of others, pushing out through the main door of the hall. They were jostling each other, jostling the crowd, their heavy stupid faces eager and single-minded. Last year they'd been in Year 12; now they worked the fishing boats and the shire garbage trucks or hung around the streets.

Louis didn't believe it about Tilly, didn't want to believe it. He darted through the crowd, taking a shortcut across the dance floor, scattering the dancers.

He burst into the darkness outside. He seemed to be in a partial world, suddenly: distant streetlights instead of dusty chandeliers; murmurs instead of shouts; only men, no women; beery smells drifting by his nostrils, not perfume; and cigarettes burning, bright red eyes in the shadows.

He walked quickly, following Matthews and the others around the side of the hall, past a rainwater tank and a toilet block, to the carpark. The park was full, windscreens reflecting the wintry moon, ducoed metal drawing the dew from the air.

Then he lost them. It was too dark. He tried to follow their voices and their footsteps. The carpark was full of muddy potholes and half-submerged rocks.

A car door slammed somewhere.

Giggles in the darkness.

A bottle flew and shattered at Louis' feet.

Someone squealed, then giggled, and there was a slap and then quietness again.

A man and a woman emerged from a car and staggered back to the hall.

Then nothing for several seconds. Louis stood perfectly still, waiting and listening.

Someone screamed. It was not a scream of delight but of fear. Heavy male voices drowned it out:

'Come on, slag.'

'Yeah, open the door.'

'We've all got five bucks for you.'

'Won't pay you anything at all if you don't open this bloody door.'

Louis rushed forward. He tripped and stumbled headlong between the nose of one car and the tail of another, putting out his hands to break his fall, feeling the bolt on a towbar slice his thumb to the bone.

He stood again and wrapped his handkerchief around the cut.

Someone shouted, 'Come on, you bitch, don't be a tease. Open this bloody door.'

Louis found Matthews and the others clustered around Mr Chatters' Austin truck. They were tugging so hard on the door handles that the truck was rocking on its tired springs.

'*Leave her alone*,' he yelled.

They stopped. They stared at him. 'Who the hell are you?'

Louis came closer. 'Leave her alone!' His voice came out as a squeak this time.

They laughed. One of them said, 'It's the Deane kid.' Another called, laughing, 'Hey, mate, go home to your mum, it's your bedtime.'

Louis felt hard and dangerous. He crouched,

ready to fly at them. This time his voice didn't betray him. 'Clear out. Leave her alone.'

There was a ratchety sound as Tilly lowered a side window of the truck. She looked scared. 'Louis, go and get help. Don't fight them, go and get help.'

He shouted back, 'Okay. Wind up your window again.'

Brett Matthews and Justin Kolodny and the others looked at each other in disgust. 'Ah, let's forget it, not worth the hassle,' one of them said.

As they turned to leave, there was a roar of anger in the darkness. A low, heavy, unstoppable shape charged amongst them. It was as if a train had ploughed into a herd of cattle. Slam, slap, punch, kick, *oof*, *ouch*, a long *ohhh* of pain.

It was Mr Chatters. As they retreated, limping and moaning, he shouted, 'Cowards. Get out of here the lot of you.' He aimed a kick at Brett Matthews. 'Go on, you piece of shit, clear out before I throttle you.' He saw Louis, rushed at him, arms windmilling wildly. 'Clear off, go on.'

Louis ran.

SEVENTEEN

There was a two-week break now, before the start of the last term. Time dragged for Louis. He wanted to visit Tilly Chatterton, but daren't risk it. Mr Chatters would run him off the place, and there was no reason to suppose that Tilly would want to see him. He spent time hanging around the shopping centre, hoping to spot her, but she didn't appear. Meanwhile his self-loathing grew. Words swirled around in his head, and he boiled them down to one irreducible charge: what he'd done might one day be forgiven, and sooner or later forgotten, but it could never be erased.

He was desperate for distractions. But what? There was only Craven and Bird, and he didn't want to spend time with them.

He counted his pocket money. He had enough money for one trip up to the city. Eight hours later, he was back in Bass Beach feeling worse than before. Perhaps he'd changed, or his friends had changed. Too much time had gone by. When Louis talked scathingly about Bass Beach and the school, his friends were no more than politely interested. And their own talk of life in Louis' old school was full of names and incidents that meant little to him. It's as if we're describing unfamiliar times and places to each other, he thought. Except for the fact that we used to hang out together, there's no common ground between us any more. As the day progressed, their conversations began to dwindle away, and by the time Louis had to catch the train back to Bass Beach, his old friends were leaving him out of their conversations altogether.

At home, things weren't much better. Steph

would leave the house at 5 a.m. to pick up, sort and later deliver the mail, and her afternoons were split between writing and attending a poetry workshop at the TAFE College in Fenwick. By the end of two weeks she'd written ten poems and sent them off to literary magazines. She hummed a lot. Life in Bass Beach suited her.

Meanwhile Carl had been commissioned to make five hundred bread crocks for a chain of cottage-craft gift shops. He was flat out working to meet the order. Soon Louis was sick of the sight of bread crocks on the back verandah, hundreds of them, all alike, pale yellow, heavy and bulbous, like the giant spores of a mutant plant creeping over the house.

And Meg? She'd been transformed by love. She was less slangy, sharp or dismissive now. Bass Beach had become a warmer, more positive place for her. Sometimes she'd even stop what she was doing and hug Louis and ask him how he was doing, but she would rarely listen to his replies, so he knew she was in a world of her own. She'd spin away, humming, her eyes dreamy, and he'd feel betrayed.

There was another unfortunate consequence of Meg's new state: Craven and Bird. Whenever Craven's brother visited Meg, coolly bored and distant, Craven and Bird would tag along with him. Louis tried hiding, tried slipping out and over the back fence, but somehow Craven and Bird always found him.

Bird was lost without Craven, and both seemed to be lost without Louis. They'd crowd into his bedroom and gaze around at his posters, his computer games, his Terry Pratchett collection. 'Show us your Web site again,' they'd say, and watch Louis tap the keys, watch the shapes and colours swirl, dissolve and alter shape on the monitor screen. They were transfixed. It was as though Louis possessed a powerful magic gift. 'How many hits?' they'd ask, and Louis would show them. He'd scan the messages. People were always dropping in and out. Mathilde had stopped corresponding with the other fans some time ago.

But Craven and Bird would also get restless and want to do something. They seemed to think that Louis held the key to their happiness, that he was full of nerve and daring.

'Let's have a smoke.'

Louis didn't want to smoke.

'Let's pinch some swapcards at the newsagent's.'

Louis wasn't interested.

'Why don't we let the air out of Old Valentine's tyres.'

Old Valentine had made the mistake of living in Bass Beach. Mad, Louis thought. If you were a policeman or a teacher, *never* live where you worked.

'Don't feel like it,' he said.

'You're a drag, you know that?' Craven said.

Then Bird said, 'We could get Tilly Chatterton to do a strip for us. My place. Mum and Dad aren't home. I know where I can get hold of ten dollars.'

'Yeah,' Craven said. 'What about it, Lou?'

Louis felt himself go hot and tight and choked inside. He'd spent the holidays trying not to think about Tilly Chatterton, her pain, his clumsiness, the town thugs yanking at the doors of the Austin truck, Mr Chatters' angry boots and fists.

Why *had* Tilly gone outside to sit in the truck?

Had she been waiting for someone?

Who?

Why?

And how come Mr Chatters had appeared? Was he chasing off Matthews and the others, or was he checking up on Tilly? Louis went cold. Maybe Tilly *had* gone off with guys before.

No. He didn't believe it.

Craven said again, 'Come on, Louis. Let's do it. She's game for anything.'

'Leave her alone.'

'You're not still soft on her?'

'Leave her alone,' Louis said again.

Craven and Bird sulked. 'Piss weak, Lou.'

Louis stared away, stiff and chafing.

Bird said, 'Me and you'll go and see her, Crave. Forget old wimpface here.'

'Yeah.'

Louis stood, bunched his fists, and launched himself at them. They began to fight. But there was no space for a fight. They knocked against the desk. The bed caught them behind their knees. They had no room to swing their fists or kick or charge. All they could do was push and shove and grapple uselessly, filling the air with grunts and gasps. It was an inconclusive fight. It left them winded and hating, and Louis felt his claustrophobia closing in.

He gasped, 'Just leave Tilly alone.'

'It must be love,' Craven said.

Louis cried out and reached for Craven's neck. 'Chill out, Lou,' Bird said, blocking him.

They left after that.

The only good thing about those two weeks was the weather. As Louis' corner of the world edged into spring, blossoms appeared, lawns needed cutting, the roadside verges were choked with grass, and birds began to nest. Carl said, one afternoon, 'We've been neglecting the bush block. Let's go.'

They drove out there. The place had transformed itself in their absence. There were no fruit tree skeletons any more, no grassless muddy patches around the old house. Carl scratched his head critically. 'Needs a good mowing.'

'And whipper-snipping,' Meg said.

Steph nodded at a patch of grass behind the house. 'This would be a good time to start a vegie patch.'

Craven's brother was with them, glued to Meg's hip. He uttered one of the longest sentences Louis had ever heard from him: 'I can help.'

They all chirped on and Louis began to kick at the dusty ground. There was a brisk wind in the trees. Above the sound of it he could hear a regular mechanical rattle. He looked across at the windmill. The revolving vanes were blurred with speed and the whole structure seemed to be shaking itself apart.

'The windmill doesn't look right,' he said.

Carl had his hair down today and pushed both hands back through it. 'Why can't life be simple?'

'We'll have to get it fixed,' Steph said. 'I'll need pump water for the vegie patch.'

Carl sighed. 'More bloody expense.'

'Mr Chatters is the expert,' Craven's brother said.

That was the last thing Louis wanted to hear.

EIGHTEEN

It wasn't until the end of the second week of the break that Mr Chatters could come out to fix the windmill. He arranged to meet them there one day after lunch. It was a warm day, the sky clear. But a strong wind began to gust during the morning, and Louis hoped that Mr Chatters would phone and cancel, saying it was too dangerous to work under such conditions.

Louis waited through the long morning. He logged on to his Web site, read, twiddled his thumbs. No phone call came. He found Carl in the kitchen with Meg and Craven's brother. 'Dad, I've got things to do today. Can't Meg go out to the block with you?'

'I don't care which one of you comes out.'

But Meg said, 'Sorry, Andy and I are going to a film today.'

Meg and Craven's brother went around stuck together flank to flank like Siamese twins. Louis saw them swaying, Meg gazing up at Andy's moody face, and said sourly, 'Can I come to the flicks with you?'

'I thought you said you had things to do today?'

Louis muttered, 'Maybe Steph can go out with you, Dad.'

'Your mother's been up since five this morning. Leave her be.'

It was no good: Louis would have to face Mr Chatters again.

When he and Carl arrived at the bush block after lunch, the faded red Austin was already there, parked near the windmill, Mr Chatters leaning against the wheel arch, watching them. He looked smaller, frailer, under the dome of the sky. He wore khaki work pants, a sleeveless grey shirt and unbendable black boots, and the felt hat pushed back on his forehead was marked by greasy fingermarks and a high tide of hair oil and sweat.

He continued to watch as Louis and Carl climbed out of the car and approached him through the long grass. He had all the patience in the world, rolling one of his fags, his head cocked, a sober, assessing expression on his face. Louis cringed inside. He waited for Mr Chatters to point his thick finger and say, 'Carl, that boy of yours is scum. Get him out of my sight.'

Instead, Mr Chatters nodded, then jerked his head at the windmill. 'I thought there might be a break in one of the rods. That's the last thing you need, especially near the bottom of the shaft, because it means you have to pull out all the rods to get to it.' He went on to explain that he was familiar with their bore, for he'd fixed it for the previous owner. Its dark mysteries seemed to make him shiver. 'A deep shaft,' he said, 'cold, ancient water.'

Louis' father nodded as if he understood. 'So, what *is* the problem?'

Again that jerk of the head. 'See how freely she's spinning? Stripped a cog, most likely.'

They looked up. The windmill, like a small, unadorned Eiffel Tower, was still spinning rapidly—a sign, Louis now realised, that there was no resistance, that the pumping rods were not hauling the deeply buried water to the surface. The rudder pointed south, for the wind was from the north, and the vanes were flashing as the sun caught them.

'Worn out, like the rest of us,' Mr Chatters said.

'Been here since the year dot,' Carl agreed.

Mr Chatters finished poking stray flecks of tobacco into his newly rolled cigarette, lit it, drew in a lungful of smoke, and took it away from his mouth again, the fag pinched between the ends of his thumb and forefinger, the coal-tip millimetres from his palm. Louis had had it explained to him once, that odd way of holding a cigarette. Mr Chatters must have served in the army once upon a time, back when he was scarcely out of his teens, and probably stood sentry duty in the long dark jungle nights, risking a smoke, keeping the glowing tip hidden from enemy snipers in the nearby trees.

Finally Mr Chatters said, 'Well, better make a start.'

'Unfortunately I've got to fire a few pots this afternoon,' Carl said. 'Can you manage without me for the next hour or two?'

Mr Chatters examined the tip of his cigarette. 'Sure.'

'I'll be back before five with any luck.'

'Suit yourself.'

Carl swung his face down to Louis'. 'You stay here, son. Help Mr Chatterton.'

And then he was gone. Louis burned with the betrayal. He and Mr Chatters eyed each other doubtfully. They shared a difficult history—Tilly, the haircuts, and the incident in the shire hall carpark, and Louis expected bitterness or anger. Finally, though, Mr Chatters simply shrugged and gathered his tools together, saying, as he headed for the base of the windmill, 'Water in the bag. Help yourself.'

A jute waterbag, dusty, oil-streaked, damp and prickly, was wired to the snout of the Austin. Louis uncorked it and poured water down his throat. There was a taste of metal, of dust, oil and jute.

Mr Chatters began to climb the windmill. Louis idled at the base of it for some time, but didn't seem to be needed so he wandered back to the Austin and climbed into the cab. More dust, a shotgun shell, a torn Larry and Stretch western paperback novella, a half bottle of St Agnes brandy, sandwiches in greaseproof paper and a thermos of tea in a cane basket, and a trashy magazine gritty with road dust, half of the pinups torn out. Louis settled down to read. Somewhere in the background metal rang against metal as Mr Chatters began to work on the windmill head.

Then there was a faint movement of the truck. A shape blocked the sunlight at the open side window. Louis looked up.

NINETEEN

He gaped. 'Tilly.'

'Hello, Louis.'

She stood on the running board, looking in at him, her forearms resting on the window ledge. She had a book in one hand. It was the Pratchett novel he'd given her.

'I didn't know you were here.'

She looked away, pointing. 'I've been reading down at the dam, out of the wind.'

She stepped off, disappearing from sight for a moment before she opened the door and climbed in next to him. There wasn't much room in the cab; she was very close, and Louis found himself stammering, 'I'm sorry about everything.'

She glanced at him coolly. 'Such as?'

'Telling you I couldn't be your partner for the Polonaise.'

She shrugged. 'It doesn't matter.'

'People were saying things about you and I shouldn't have listened.'

'Happens all the time.'

They were silent. For Louis it was the most awkward silence he'd ever endured, but Tilly didn't seem fussed one way or the other. He struggled to speak, his cheeks on fire. 'Is any of it true?'

Again that cool, level look. 'What do you think?'

Louis glanced away. 'I don't know.'

'Louis, look at me.'

He looked.

'Do you really think I could have done all those things?'

He found himself looking past her wild hair, the rings and the studs. Those things were only dressing up, he did it himself. Maybe she simply wanted to look different from the people around her, just as he did, but got judged harshly for it.

'No,' he said.

She glanced away. After a while she said, 'Your mum and dad—they're kind of hippies, aren't they?'

'Kind of.'

'So are mine. Long hair, beads, crappy music, lots of hanging around smoking dope.'

'Mine don't do dope.'

'Lucky you.'

She was silent, looking back down the years of her life. 'They started growing and selling it.'

Louis understood. 'They got caught?'

She nodded. 'They're in jail.'

'That's why you came to stay with Mr Chatters?'

'Yes.'

'You weren't expelled?'

She was sharp. *'Louis.'*

'Sorry.'

'Our photos were in the local paper,' she said. 'A lot of finger-pointing at school and in the street. Most of the kids I knew weren't allowed to hang around with me any more, only the kids you saw me with in Fenwick that time. We had to move house. Then the trial and Mum and Dad got sent to jail for six months. Anyone would think they were criminal masterminds or something. They're not bad, just a bit hopeless, their heads in a different place. I mean, all they did was grow a few plants in the garage.'

She watched him for a while. There was no sign of the pain he'd seen in her eyes two weeks ago. She was much more sure of herself now, as though she'd grown up and outstripped him. The whistling wind blew. The little truck rocked with it.

'I was disappointed,' Tilly said finally. 'I thought you could be my friend.'

He said with feeling, 'I still *can*.'

She shrugged. 'Maybe.'

'I'll make it up to you, Tilly.'

He could hear himself, his desperation, and didn't like it. He felt small. He tried to rally, and to put himself in a better light. 'At the Ball I came out to see if you were all right,' he said.

She flashed around sharply. 'No you didn't. You came out to see if I was having sex with those morons. You came out to see if the things everyone was saying were true.'

Louis felt close to tears. She knew him inside and out.

She said, 'Do you want to know why I left the hall after the Polonaise?'

'You'd had enough of the stares and whispers.'

'Partly, but they can all go and jump in the lake. No, mostly it was because I didn't know what I'd do if you'd come over and asked me for a dance. I didn't want to have to talk to you.'

'Oh,' he said, looking away from her.

She seemed to relent. 'But you were upset when you saw those idiots trying to get at me. That's nice.'

'I tried to stop them,' Louis said. 'I shouted at them.'

'Thank you.'

'But your uncle thinks I was part of it.'

Tilly shook her head. 'Not any more. I explained what happened.'

Louis relaxed a little in his seat. The seconds ticked by. It was warm and dusty smelling in the old truck. After a while, he became aware of the greater silence outside. Mr Chatters had ceased bashing metal against metal at the top of the windmill tower. Even the wind had dropped.

Louis turned to Tilly. He had to ask. 'When you ran away the other day, was it because I—'

She nodded abruptly, as if she wanted him to shut up.

But he didn't think he could withstand another silence. 'Where did you go?'

'I took a bus to Sydney. I stayed in the YWCA hostel while I looked for a job.'

Louis wondered if he'd ever have the nerve or know-how to do the things that she'd done. 'Why did you come home?'

'I didn't choose to. The police came around one day and showed my photo at the reception desk.'

'Did you get into trouble?'

'Uncle Roly and Auntie Jess came to fetch me back. They were so relieved to have me home again, they didn't tell me off.' She gestured dismissively. 'It was a stupid thing to do, running away over such a little matter.'

That made Louis feel that *he* was little, and he wasn't getting much encouragement from what she was saying, but still he pressed on. 'It took a lot of guts to come to the Ball after that.'

'Uncle Roly was just fantastic. He said to me, "Hold your head up", so I did.'

'I don't know how I could have been so shitty to you,' Louis said.

Tilly seemed to examine his face. 'Louis, I'm not interested in how low you can sink, only in how high you can reach.' She paused. 'Uncle Roly said that to me one day.'

They fell silent again. Tilly relaxed in the cracked and sunken seat and that seemed to bring her a few centimetres closer to Louis. Soon she was only a handspan away from his thighs and shoulders. It was as if they were both edging toward the midpoint of the bench seat.

He touched the cover of the Terry Pratchett on her lap. 'Are you enjoying the book?'

Her smile was very wide. 'Mathilde likes it, thank you.'

Louis stared at her. He found his voice: 'That was *you*?'

'I didn't know if you would twig or not. I tried to give you clues, but I guess they were too obscure.'

'I always looked forward to the Mathilde messages,' Louis said. 'They were clever.'

More silence. Anything could tip it one way or the other.

Louis became aware of the breathing first, a sound full of intense pain and effort. He turned his head.

Mr Chatters filled the driver's door window of the little truck. His features were clenched in a kind of fury, the skin pale and stretched painfully tight over the bones of his face. The words came out as if he were strangling powerful emotions in his throat.

'Out,' he said. *'Now.'*

TWENTY

Louis didn't move. He felt emboldened by his conversation with Tilly. He wasn't going to let Mr Chatters get the wrong end of the stick again. 'We aren't doing anything,' he said. 'We're just talking.'

Mr Chatters clenched his teeth. His face was very white. *'Please. Now.'*

Tilly leaned across Louis. 'We're only talking, Uncle Roly. Honest.'

Mr Chatters' eyes rolled back in his head. He

swayed a little. Then his left hand floated into view. It was streaming blood. *'Please.'*

Tilly cried out. Mr Chatters' ring and middle fingers had been torn away at the lower knuckles. Louis saw the blood pump, down Mr Chatters' wrist and his tough, corded forearm, to drip in pulse-beats from the point of his elbow. The voice was a croak now. *'Please. Help me.'*

Louis clambered out, held the door open, and put an arm around Mr Chatters' waist. Tilly reached across from the passenger seat and grabbed her uncle's right hand and hauled him into the driver's seat. The door slammed.

'I—,' Louis said, as if to step on to the running board.

They ignored him. With his good hand, Mr Chatters pulled the starter knob, crashed the old truck into first gear, and steered bumpingly away toward the road gate. Louis stood watching helplessly. He saw the Austin creep through the open gate and begin to trundle down the lane to the main road.

The world seemed empty, suddenly. There was only the endless sky, the spring grasses, and Louis himself, standing alone.

After a while, he wandered away to the base of the windmill, following the blood splashed like red beads on the grass and balled in the greasy dirt at the base of the mill. That's where he found the open pocketknife. Louis recognised it as the one Mr Chatters wore in a black leather pouch on his belt. The blade was open. Blood smeared the gleaming metal and clots of it were lumped here and there on the blade and the handle.

Louis looked up, and, in his mind's eye, saw the wind suddenly gust and shift direction. The vanes spin, and cogs turn, trapping Mr Chatters' fingers. Maybe he loses his footing, too, and swings outwards from the rung of the ladder, putting a tearing strain on his mangled hand. What can he do? Of what use are Louis and Tilly, down in the cab of his little Austin truck? He calls, but there is the wind to compete with, the tricky scrapes and eddies of the wind in the grass and the tossing tree-tops, and no one hears his cries for help.

And so he reaches back with his right hand and snaps open the leather pouch and fumbles open the blade—did he use his teeth?—and finally saws through flesh and bone to set himself free.

Perhaps he'd realised that the fingers were beyond saving even if someone *had* been there to climb up and free them.

Perhaps he'd been dizzy with pain and blood loss, and knew that he had to free himself immediately, before he fainted or his right hand failed him, for then he'd plummet to his death.

Louis shivered. Hours seemed to pass, but it was only a few minutes. He thought, absurdly, that at least Mr Chatters hadn't mangled his scissors hand. He tried to imagine what Mr Chatters' left hand would look like once it was healed, cupping the back of his head, praising its shapeliness. Will I be able to sense the missing fingers? he wondered.

The wind picked up again. Louis' thoughts turned treacherous. No one has time for me. No one needs me. The world's turning without me. Mr Chatters won't want to cut hair again, or fix windmills. He and Tilly don't need anyone. They've proved that. They look after one another.

As he kicked at the onion weed, Louis heard

a faint, wheezy cry above the whistling wind. A bird?

No. A horn.

He climbed the windmill tower until he could look down on the lane beyond the screen of roadside trees and blackberry thickets. The old red truck was stalled at an angle halfway down the lane, nosing into the ditch. Louis felt a wetness on his fingers. Blood. He looked at the metal ladder, then up at the machinery cogs. A mess of blood and gristle. He began to sway. After several seconds, in which he almost succumbed to the black light swirling about his head, he fought down his panic and clambered to the ground, missing steps, barking his shins as he went.

At the bottom, he ran. He fell, picked himself up. There were snags concealed in the spring grass—burrows and fissures, abandoned fencing wire, and reefs of rock. Then he was at the fenceline and slipping between the wires. He ran.

It was quieter in the lane, between the funnelling trees. The Austin was burbling quietly, oily exhaust smoke chugging into the air. Otherwise, there was no sign of life, not until Louis reached the cab and hauled the door open and found Tilly bearing the unconscious weight of her uncle. They manoeuvred him away from the steering-wheel and then it was Louis' turn to crash the gears and get them out of trouble. At one point, Mr Chatters groaned and seemed to search for something in the air with his good hand. Louis reached out and clasped it until they reached the corner. That seemed to soothe Mr Chatters, Tilly holding on to his bloodied hand, Louis to the other, spreading the comfort and peace across the little space.

TWENTY-ONE

They got as far as the outskirts of town.

First there were flashing blue and red lights, then the brief yelp of a siren, and Louis saw an unmarked black car in the rear-view mirror.

'Police.'

'Sergeant Penny?'

'No.'

'Keep going,' Tilly said urgently. She looked out; they were adjacent to the racecourse. 'The hospital's not far now.'

Louis pressed his foot down on the

accelerator, thinking: This is going to be a *low*-speed car chase.

The siren howled this time and the black car swooped past the Austin and into the kerb, forcing Louis to press down on the spongy brake pedal and steer up on to the footpath. The engine promptly stalled. He began to tremble.

A young policeman got out, moving slowly, grimly adjusting his sunglasses as he swaggered toward the Austin. He stopped at Louis' window and jerked his thumb.

'Out.'

Louis wound down the window. 'It's an emergency.'

The policeman's jaw dropped. 'You're just a kid. Out, come on, don't stuff around.'

Tilly leaned across and shouted. 'We're going to the hospital!'

The policeman looked at them doubtfully, as though Tilly might be about to give birth and Louis were the young father. Then he stepped on to the running board for a better look and saw Mr Chatters, pale and still across Tilly's lap, his blood leaking onto the knees of her jeans.

The grimness vanished. 'Leave the jalopy. I'll take you in the car.'

It gave him the chance to use the siren again.

After Mr Chatters had been admitted at Casualty and wheeled away by an aide, Louis and Tilly used the telephone. There was no answer at Louis' house: Carl was probably firing pots in the backyard and Steph and Meg were out. When Tilly tried Mrs Chatters, she got the answering machine and left a message. 'I forgot she was going out today. It's just you and me, Louis.'

They looked at each other in the little waiting room with its wall-mounted television set silently broadcasting Oprah, its handful of people sprawled in shabby plastic chairs, and Tilly made a small gesture with her arms, lifting them out from her sides. Louis stepped toward her. He took another step, into her embrace, and all at once the old badness leaked away.

For the next two hours they sat, knees together, hands entwined. Sometimes they murmured, remembering comic incidents from school, Mr Chatters' adventures with the Austin or certain prickly personalities on the Terry Pratchett Web site, and sometimes they simply watched their hands, which seemed to have a separate life, twisting and stroking. They weren't aware of the other people who came and went and smiled or frowned at them.

At five o'clock they were allowed in to see Mr Chatters. His finger stumps were bulky with red-spotted gauze bandages, and he looked pale and hollow-cheeked, the skin stretched tight in pain and shock.

He brightened when he saw them at the door.

'You kids,' he said, beckoning them with his right hand.

They drew chairs to the side of his bed and told him about the policeman.

'He didn't book you?'

'No,' Louis said.

The good hand squeezed Louis' forearm. 'You came through for me. Thank you.'

'That's okay.'

'Have you thought of a job for the summer?'

Louis hadn't. For months he'd thought his summer would be spent up in the city, with his old friends, but that wasn't likely now. The city seemed to be a long way back in the past. 'What kind of job?'

'Working for me.'

'Sweeping the floor?'

'Handing me tools when I fix windmills.'

'Uncle Roly,' Tilly said, 'you're not fixing windmills again.'

'Why not?'

'Your hand.'

'I've still got one good hand and most of the fingers on the other one.'

'I'd lose my head for heights after what you've been through,' Louis said.

'Son, if you fall off a bike or a horse, you get right back on it,' Mr Chatters said.

Another one of his sayings for managing life. 'What about Tilly?' Louis said. 'We could both help you.'

A silence fell. Tilly looked away. Mr Chatters looked away.

Finally Tilly took a deep breath and looked at Louis. 'Mum and Dad appealed against their jail sentence,' she said. 'They get out soon. They want to take me to Queensland or somewhere.'

She looked at him helplessly. 'Until today it hadn't seemed necessary to tell you.'

TWENTY-TWO

It was early summer, two days before Christmas, and Louis was at the top of the windmill tower on the bush block, wearing a hat, a long-sleeved shirt and plenty of sunblock. Like Mr Chatters, he wore a safety harness. Mr Chatters' toolkit was around his waist. Mr Chatters would say 'adjustable wrench' or 'grease gun' and Louis would pass them to him like a nurse in a surgery.

The winter and spring had been dry. All of the orchards, vineyards, pony clubs and hobby farms of the Peninsula were tapping into the underground water for their plants and animals, and so Mr Chatters was always being called out to repair windmills, but in this instance it was to prepare the bush block for auction. Louis looked down at the apples in the old trees, still small and sour. He glanced at the house, which Carl had tired of renovating. They'd all decided that they were happy living behind the shop, so there was no point in hanging on to the bush block, and they could do with the money.

'Oil can,' Mr Chatters said.

It wasn't such a bad job. Louis earned a few dollars an hour and kept himself occupied—though there were times when he found his mind wandering, and Mr Chatters would bring him back with a sharp clap of his hands and an 'Oi, wake up!'.

Louis' mind was wandering now.

He'd been there when Tilly's parents came to fetch her. It had been the most miserable day of his life. He'd blinked away tears, Tilly had sobbed inconsolably, Mr Chatters had looked on stonily and Tilly's parents, ashamed and defeated-looking from their time in prison, had kept their eyes on the ground.

'I'll never forget you,' Tilly shouted, as the car drove away.

'Write!' Louis shouted back. 'Email!'

From whatever rainforest commune they're taking you to.

But she didn't write or email him, even though they hadn't gone to Queensland but to another part of the city.

'Pliers,' snapped Mr Chatters.

Louis passed him the pliers. Mr Chatters' left hand looked odd, as though the missing fingers were folded permanently into the palm. Mr Chatters didn't seem to know what to do with his hand when he wasn't using it, and kept it tucked in his pocket or under his right arm as if afraid that it might float free and scare little children.

Below them the new truck gave a soft ping as it flexed minutely in the sun. It was a small, white Daihatsu, more comfortable and reliable than the Austin, but already missing both wing mirrors. The front bumper bar was dented, and yesterday Mr Chatters had dropped a spanner on to the windscreen, cracking it badly.

Sure, the Austin had been due for the scrapheap, but later rather than sooner if Louis hadn't been pulled over by that policeman. Sergeant Penny might have overlooked the Austin's faults, but the younger man hadn't. On the day of the accident he'd gone straight back from the hospital and slapped a roadworthy infringement notice on the windscreen.

'She's too far gone to fix up,' Mr Chatters had said, and he'd bought the Daihatsu.

Gone, but not forgotten. Louis had posted a message on his Web site, apologising for straying from the topic but asking did anyone out there know where he could get a bonnet ornament for a 1950 Austin truck? A week later a man emailed him from Wales: he had one in pristine condition, no charge, thank you for a wonderful Web site.

So that was Mr Chatters' Christmas present taken care of. Louis had bought a CD for Meg, a famous-women-writers diary for Steph, and a subscription to a surfing magazine for Carl, in the hope that Carl would actually get out on the surfboard instead of allowing it to fade in the verandah sun.

And for Tilly he'd bought the Christmas-release Terry Pratchett novel.

He'd tried to forget her. It hadn't been easy. All Mr Chatters would do was growl 'Bad business' if Louis asked about her, and Steph and Carl weren't much use, so that left Meg. She'd broken off with Andy Craven and had plenty of advice to give about relationships.

'Move on,' she said, 'like I'm doing.'

Andy Craven had spent so much energy being cool that in the end he'd cooled her right off. 'All that scowling,' she said, 'and looking away into the distance as if he had more important things on his mind. I got sick of repeating myself to get his attention.'

She'd got his attention, all right. Now Andy Craven was always ringing her tearfully or hanging around to get a glimpse of her. 'Like he's had a personality change,' she said one day, watching him in fascination through the window of the shop.

From Louis' point of view, the main benefit

of the breakup was that he now saw less of Craven and Bird.

'I'm not saying that you have to forget Tilly,' Meg had advised, all those weeks ago, 'just remember her differently. You've both moved on.'

'I feel empty.'

'So fill yourself up,' she'd said crossly.

How?

At first he'd thrown himself into school work. He got an A minus for Old Valentine's stupid essay and by the end of the year had come top of Year 8. But still he'd felt dissatisfied, and turned to the Web site. Soon it consumed all of his spare time and took the edge off his loneliness. He enjoyed being connected to like-minded strangers—except that they weren't strangers. He'd see their words crawl across the screen and feel close to them. They were as obsessed with Terry Pratchett's characters and plots as he was, and were forever testing one another.

Mr Chatters poked his shoulder. 'Oi! Pass me the wrench.'

Louis shook off the daydream and passed the wrench.

But the day was warm. He was happy. He slipped into the dream again, saving the best part till last.

He'd been miserable until a couple of weeks ago, when a strange message appeared on the Web site:

Keep the faith, Louis.

Other messages had followed:

My name means 'might', 'strength' and 'strife'.

I was William the Conqueror's wife.

Save the last waltz for me, Louis.

His skin tingled now, just as it had when he'd realised who it was. *Mathilde.* He'd even performed an Internet search and confirmed the name's history and meaning.

Meanwhile Mathilde was getting plenty of replies from the other visitors to the Web site:

This site is reserved for discussions of Terry Pratchett's books only. Please keep your remarks relevant, or sign off now.

Mathilde had replied:

Oh, but they are relevant. Are you ready for me, Louis?

Mr Chatters' fingers snapped. 'Oi, stop talking to yourself.'

Louis blinked. 'What did I say?'

'Something about being ready.'

Louis blushed.

'I need grease.'

Louis passed him the grease gun.

So, Tilly was in contact at last. But how should he reply? To the flesh-and-blood Tilly, or to the Web presence, Mathilde? And where should he send the Christmas present?

And what did she mean, *Are you ready?* Ready for what?

Just then Louis noticed a movement in the corner of his eye. A black car was creeping up the driveway from the lane. 'We've got company,' he said.

They watched the car stop. The driver's door opened. It was the young policeman.

'Oh no.'

'What?' Mr Chatters demanded.

Louis told him.

When the policeman was at the base of the windmill, Mr Chatters roared down, 'Don't tell me you've come to roadworthy my new truck?'

The young policeman pushed back his cap,

removed his sunglasses and grinned up at them. 'She'll keep. I've come about Matilda.'

'What about her?'

'She's in the car.'

Mr Chatters started to climb down the ladder. Frowning and bewildered, Louis followed him.

'I found her hitching on the freeway,' the policeman explained. 'Said she'd run away and was coming to live with you.' He paused. 'How's the hand?'

'Forget the flaming hand,' Mr Chatters said. 'Where is she?'

'In the car.'

'This time she *stays* with me,' Mr Chatters said.

'That's not my concern. I rang her parents. They didn't even know she was gone.'

The police car was fitted with smoky glass. Louis watched the front passenger door swing open. Tilly got out. She was nervous, trying to work a hopeful grin onto her face, but when Mr Chatters held out his arms she started to run, and flung herself against him.

Louis watched them uncertainly. Then she broke away and beckoned him. 'You, too.'

He felt her arm go around his waist. Her

breath was warm on his cheek. Would she be allowed to stay this time? Mathilde equals Matilda equals Tilly, he thought. He should have spotted it before.

'I got your message,' he said.